20 TALES

OF

CALIFORNIA

Hector Lee

Rayve Productions
Windsor, California

Published by   Rayve Productions Inc.
                POB 726
                Windsor CA 95492

Illustrated by Sam Sirdofsky

Printed in the United States of America

Library of Congress Cataloging-in-Publication:

Lee, Hector, 1908 — 1992
        20 tales of California / Hector Lee.
            p.   cm.
        Rev. ed. of: Tales of California from the history and folklore of
    the Far West. 1974.
        ISBN 1-877810-62-2 (alk. paper)
        1. California--History--Anecdotes.   2. California--Biography--
Anecdotes. 3. Folklore--California.   I. Lee, Hector, 1908-1992
Tales of California from the history and folklore of the Far West.
II. Title
F861.6L44 1997   97-28925
979.4--dc21
CIP

Previous versions of the stories in this book were published in 1974 by Hector Lee in his book titled *Tales of California*. The late Dr. Lee was past president of the California Folklore Society and emeritus professor of English at Sonoma State University.

To Dorothy DuVander Johnson, whose boundless enthusiasm for life and joy in sharing her family's story of the Luffenholtz fire inspired us to publish this book.

- The Publisher

Introduction

These stories are drawn from folklore and local history of California. Most of them are about real people. They are essentially true insofar as the historical facts can be verified, but some of them are folklore, too, insofar as the folk remember the truth or have fashioned it into a local legend to retain the "essential truth" that may be closer to the spirit of a time, place, or person than the actual fact. They represent old times in California and symbolize the great Western adventure.

The late Dr. Hector Lee was well known throughout the West as an entertaining storyteller and speaker on western history and folklore. He was a distinguished educator and at one time the president of the California Folklore Society.

Contents

Appendix

Last Train From Luffenholtz

A forest fire is a wild thing, rebellious and terrible. It is an evil monster that lays waste and cripples and kills. When you fight it, it fights back and then breaks loose, if it can, to devastate and kill again. The people of the big woods know about forest fires, and they fear and hate them. And if a whole town is burned away, it is remembered and talked about for a long time — like Luffenholtz. There's nothing left of the old town now but memories. If you went through there you probably wouldn't even want to stop. A few old burnt stumps hidden by vines, and here and there the rubble of long neglected stepping stones and foundation rocks overgrown with ferns and native mountain shrubbery are all that remain to mark the graveyard of dead houses that were once homes and a dead street that once wore the footprints of the people who lived there. The town even had a name once, but most people have forgotten what it was.

But before the town died in 1908, Luffenholtz was an important little community — at least to the lumber company and the men whose trains stopped there. Only about a hundred people made it their home, but they seemed to be happy, cheerful people. At least, that's the way it seemed to Charlie DuVander and John Atwell, who went through the town every day. DuVander was the engineer and Atwell the fireman on a little two-coach passenger train that was being operated by the Hammond Lumber Company of Eureka. The route went for a distance of about thirty miles between Eureka and Trinidad in Humboldt County. The town of Luffenholtz was three miles south of Trinidad.

Every day the little train would make its trip from Eureka to Trinidad and back. Twisting and turning around the little canyon streams, the train tooted and puffed along its winding, pleasant way. On the east were the high mountains, green with timber — the massive redwood, the fir, and pine. And along the west lay the ocean, sometimes in full view and sometimes hidden by occasional hills and wide strips of thick timber.

In the morning going up, the train crew usually saw the deer feeding along the green clearings, and occasionally a bear with her cub would amble along the side of the track or casually walk across, secure in the knowledge that the train would slow down a little to let them pass.

Threaded along this railroad line were little logging towns like Luffenholtz. It was a camp populated mostly by men who worked in the woods. A few of them had brought their wives and children in, and the place looked more like a village than a logging camp. Curtains brought color to the windows, and drying laundry fluttered in the breeze. Children scampered out from nowhere when the train passed, and John Atwell always waved at them; and Charlie DuVander usually tooted the whistle or rang the bell, a ritual that followed the same happy pattern day after day.

The summer of 1905 was hot and dry. Forest fires were beginning to break out in the mountains, and great clouds of dark smoke appeared in the sky far to the eastward. The people were particularly careful in the woods that summer. But one day as the little train was pulling out of Trinidad for its return trip, word came that a fire had broken out in the dry brush near Luffenholtz. The smoke was already beginning to rise.

As they came close to the town, Charlie and John could see the flames. It looked as though the town was completely encircled with fire. The train might make it through, with luck, but the chances were getting slimmer by the minute. They could stop and back up and get back to Trinidad, where they would be safe. That was the sensible thing to do. Charlie looked at John. He could see that the question was already in John's eyes. The wind was hot, and the smell of burning timber was everywhere. Black smoke was floating in over the tracks, and grey ash dust was settling on the hood of the engine and on his bare arm resting on the window sill. He thought of the women and children in the town ahead. He thought of the train and his responsibility to the company. He thought of the little town that was doomed, and the loggers, and their wives, and the boys and girls.

He reached for the throttle and opened it another notch. The little train lurched forward and gathered speed. John understood; he smiled and shrugged a little and pulled open the fire door of the engine and began to throw in more fuel. As they sped toward the town, they began to see the animals of the forest fleeing in panic before the rushing fire. Always the animals came toward them, and from the place into which the train must go. The deer bounded by, singly and in little groups, the does with terror in their eyes, their little fawns straining to keep up. Several bears jogged along, not stopping to look back. Rabbits zig-zagged through the brush, and a few porcupines hustled along the clearing beside the tracks. Charlie wondered again about the people of Luffenholtz.

As they entered the town, they pulled into the side-track as usual. They always met a north-bound train here and had to wait to let it pass. The switch was set, and the little train took the side-track and came to a stop. Already, Charlie could see that the town was doomed. Several houses were burning, and there was nothing to prevent the fire from taking every building in the place.

But where were the people? The town was empty, and the flames were whipping in from the eastern slopes to lick up the deserted remains. The people had all gone somewhere. That morning, it had been a normal, living town; now it was empty and dying. The people must have escaped through the woods to the west and headed for the coast, which was about a mile and a half away. Perhaps they had made it. He hoped so. Perhaps the fire had not quite encircled the town yet, and escape had been possible. But he could see flames and smoke to the west, too. The fire had certainly completed its circle by now, and the timber between the town and the ocean was already burning. Whether the people had crossed that mile and a half in time was the question.

Charlie didn't have to wait long for his answer. Into the little clearing from the west came the people. They had tried to make it through to the coast, but the fire had cut them off. Now, here they came in a mad rush toward his waiting train. The flames had turned them back to their homes to make a last desperate stand. When they saw that houses were already on fire, their hopeless fear turned to panic. Some of the big loggers ran ahead. Some of the men stayed behind to help the women. Mothers held their babies tight, running and stumbling. Some of the smaller children were crying, and there were boys and girls with solemn faces — bravely trying to help the others along.

They crossed the clearing and came to the tracks beside the train. Their panic seemed to give way to quiet resignation. They stood in a little cluster, sixty desperate faces, looking up at Charlie DuVander the engineer, as if waiting for him to find some way to save them. John Atwell took a plug of tobacco from his back pocket, bit off a chunk, and looked away from the crowd in embarrassment.

Charlie was thinking fast. He looked back up the tracks over which the train had just come. The fire had already closed in. The timber was thick and close to the tracks, and he knew that to try to go back was hopeless. He looked down the tracks ahead and wondered whether the north-bound train was coming. If the fire had closed behind that train, he knew that the engineer would be bringing it on through. To start now and meet that train a few miles down the line would mean certain death. Even if the other train had stopped, there was the likelihood that trees or burning limbs lay across the tracks, or that the trestles had burned out under the rails. To go back was impossible. The fire was raging there and cut off all possible retreat. But to remain was also out of the question.

Charlie looked at John, but the fireman was checking the steam pressure. With a wave of the hand, Charlie motioned the people to get on board. The crowd made a break for the cars and scrambled in. Suddenly they were his people, all of them — the rough men of the woods, the frightened women, the boys and girls who had waved at him from their play and who were now bravely struggling to make room for a few of their devoted cats and dogs, all of them were his people.

Without a word, John Atwell leaped from the cab and threw the switch to let them back on the main track. As the engine eased by, he swung on and began to throw in more fuel. The drive wheels spun. But the train was moving. Down the line it went, gaining speed with every notch of the throttle as Charlie opened her wide.

At the south end of town, a large cook house that stood near the tracks had been burning for some time. As the train approached, it collapsed and fell across the tracks. Charlie and John crouched back in the cab, and the engine crashed through the flaming mass, scattering burning boards like a spray of torches. A strong wind was blowing, and the fire was raging on both sides of the railroad. The heat was unbearable. The smoke was so thick it was impossible to see ahead of the engine. But with its whistle screeching, the little train raced on.

The scorching heat and the blinding smoke smothered them like a heavy blanket for nearly ten miles. Then Charlie's train came out on open land, and the fire was behind them. They came to a slow stop, and Charlie and John came down out of the cab to look over the damages. The people got out of the cars, and a great cheer went up. At last they were safe. The windows were broken and the coaches were scorched and blistered; but the train would still run, and the people of the town would get to Eureka, every one of them.

The other train that had left Eureka and should have been coming along the line had been stopped further down because a huge redwood tree had fallen across the tracks. The town of Luffenholtz was completely destroyed, and except for a few people it has faded from memory. The little train has long since vanished from the scene. And Charlie DuVander long ago made his last run.

Father Florian's Secret

It was Sunday afternoon, and almost the entire population of Sawyer's Bar had assembled at Joe Luckett's saloon and ten pin alley. Actually, the fact that it was Sunday was less responsible for the congregation of miners than another fact, which repeated itself almost as often. A death at Sawyer's Bar was a rather common occurrence in 1855 — too common to attract much notice or induce the citizens to take any serious measures to prevent it — but the subsequent funeral was always faced with unanimous solemnity.

The awesome feeling of permanence at a burial seemed to bring out a natural piety in the men. That honorable sentiment, however, somehow failed to manifest itself in time to prevent the customary chain of events that always led up to the final ceremony. And since fights occurred almost daily and a killing took place at least once a week, a cynic might say that Sawyer's Bar almost looked forward to its remorse over the consequences.

And so it had come to pass that Crevicing Jack had silenced Coyote Bill forever — the reason was scarcely worth noting, much less remembering — and after the funeral the boys had congregated in the saloon to wash away their memories of good old Bill.

But the blissful scene was marred by a stirring of dissatisfaction in the group. One of the Cave brothers had spoken the grave-side eulogy, but the desired fervor was lacking. He had been elected to this honor because the Cave brothers owned a store and some pack mules, and — except for Captain Best, who owned the hotel, and Joe Luckett the saloon keeper — he represented the most influential and esteemed stratum of society. But Artie Cave didn't have the gift of tongues, and as a funeral speaker he had failed.

"Well, I reckon a real preacher, if we'd a-had one, could of give old Bill a ticket that would of took him a lot closer to Kingdom Come than what he got," was the opinion of one crusty old miner, name of Pie Biter.

"Gentlemen," said Poker John, with the finality of an important man with his thumbs hooked in his vest, "it's time, I think, that this Bar got itself a preacher. We ought to send out for one."

And Fatty Paddy McGann, never one to pass up a chance to jump a claim or file his title to a new idea, picked up the thought quickly. "An' wasn't I sayin' only the other day, sez I, 'Boys, here we be here in so far off a place that only the Divil can find us, an' us with not even the grace of a Holy Father to put in the right word for us!' That's what I was sayin'."

"Well, now," put in the first speaker doubtfully, "I ain't so sure about us havin' no Catholic priest father in a place like this. Fer real hatin' the Devil and yellin' hell fire and brimstone, give me a Campbellite Preacher any day."

But for most of the residents of Sawyer's Bar, it mattered little which brand of Christianity arose in their midst, so long as it came in the person of an official man of God. And thus the issue was settled: the first preacher who chanced to come along would be their chosen shepherd. And with this comforting thought, the little untended flock scattered to their various mining claims and went back to work.

The camp had proved to be a profitable place for taking out the precious gold. It all started in 1850 when a Klamath Indian named Squirrel Jim had crept out of the bushes on the shores of the Salmon River in Siskiyou County and had seen a party of four white men camped along the river. With sign language he asked them what they were doing there. They explained to him that they were looking for gold, and they showed him several samples of the yellow ore that they had brought with them.

After he understood what they wanted, he led them to a spot not far away where they did find gold, lots of it, and there they set up a permanent camp, naming the place Paradise Flat. One of these four adventurers, a sea captain named Best, built a sawmill not far away to accommodate the miners who came in to work the river gravel and wanted sluice boxes.

More and more people came and settled at Paradise Flat until there wasn't room for comfort — especially when it was discovered that the very community itself — tents, shacks, and all — was sitting squarely on top of gravels that were rich in gold. So the town moved down the river a little way to another wide place in the canyon where a man named Sawyer had set up a sawmill, and they called the place Sawyer's Bar.

At this point the Salmon River was swift and cold. It came from the many mountain streams that plunged down in rapids and twisting, curling, bouncing waterfalls from the Trinity Mountains that towered against the sky to the south and west of the little valley. The Trinity Alps, they were called, and it was said that in some of the high places on the north side the snow never melted off. This was a hidden valley, almost without contact with the outer world.

In the 1850s the mining season was short. Three to four months was about all the time the miners had for work because in the winter the snows were deep, and in the spring the rivers ran high. For nearly five months of the year they were snowed in, so they had to carry in and store enough food for the quiet months. To get variety from the local venison and bear meat, they ate corned beef which they brought in from Scott Valley to the east, and they managed to have plenty of bread and beans. There were no green vegetables in the winter, but in summer they got a good supply of potatoes from Scott Valley and Yreka.

There were no roads into Sawyer's Bar. Pack mules carried the supplies in, and most of the miners came in by "shank's mare" — that is, they walked. Some came in from the northeast by way of Scott Valley, but most of them came from the coast. They got off the ships at Trinidad Bay, worked their way up to Weaverville and into the Trinity Alps, and climbed the narrow, rocky trail that twisted and zigzagged high into the very clouds, where the mighty Trinities wore away to a barren, jagged, thin edge. Then down — almost straight down, like the waterfalls — came the little trail, to level out near Coffee Creek and follow along the river bank just opposite Sawyer's Bar. Thus, every newcomer on that trail was in full view of the camp for the distance of at least half a mile across the river before he crossed the two hewn logs that made a bridge to enter the makeshift town.

And that's how it happened that the little Benedictine Monk, Father Florian Schwenninger, was seen coming before he got to Sawyer's Bar. He had come the long journey on foot over the Trinity Alps. His timely appearance just a few weeks after the camp's discussion on the subject indicated the unmistakable hand of providence. But it was even more singular that that same providence should bring it about that Fatty Paddy McGann was the first resident of the Bar to discover that the reverend Father was among them.

"Praises be!" he said, almost under his breath, as he straightened up from his shoveling to stretch his back and lift his eyes up unto the hills. "'Tis a miracle, truly." There was the frail, stooped figure of the priest, plodding along the trail with a heavy pack slung over one shoulder and a strange longish bundle over the other. "Faith, it's a holy apparition, that it is; and him comin' the long trail on foot, like the very picture of a saint, he is." And McGann hurried out to meet the priest.

So it became Paddy's great honor to usher Father Florian into Sawyer's Bar, trotting ahead of him every few moments to shout out the good news of his coming. A crowd soon gathered, and the Father was greeted with solemnity and respect. No one seemed to mind that he was a frail man, obviously in poor health, and no one paid much attention to the heavy pack he carried nor the dirt of the strenuous journey that showed on his shoes and robe.

But there was immediate curiosity, and some quiet private speculation, as to the contents of the rather long bundle he carried wrapped in torn canvas, with bits of oiled silk cloth showing through. Several pointed remarks, combined with offers to carry the mysterious package, brought a smile from the priest, but no information.

The word of the priest's coming spread quickly, and the basic facts were soon known. Father Florian Schwenninger had come to America all the way from Innsbruck, in Europe. From the Tyrolean mountains of Austria to the Trinity Alps of California was not such a far step figuratively speaking, at least, in terms of the spectacular beauty of the surroundings. But all the way from Austria, across America and through numerous mining camps in high mountains and barren deserts, this all added up to many weary steps and a distance too great to measure.

The rough miners at Sawyer's Bar took him to their hearts immediately, and he spread his gentle influence over them like a warm cloak against the winter storm. He attended to the spiritual needs of both Catholics and Protestants alike. A few miners and the town's tradesmen had brought their families, and he helped the volunteer school teacher get started with the first school.

One night as he was walking past the shack of a miner known as Rutabega Bill, he paused to listen as Bill attempted to saw out a fiddle tune on the suffering instrument for the enjoyment of five or six appreciative loungers. When a pause came in the recital Father Florian, without a word, reached out and took the fiddle from the rough hands of the miner. He sounded each string two or three times, listening intently and making the necessary adjustments of the pegs. Then he lifted the bow, and such sweet music flowed forth as the camp had never heard before. The old fiddle had been magically transformed into a violin, and it sang the deep rich harmonies of the masters; and then again it sang the light, laughing music of some gypsy camp in the old world.

After that Father Florian taught a class in music at the new school. And some of the more curious, who remembered that strange package he had carried in on his back, wondered whether it might be a musical instrument of some kind. But whatever it was, Father Florian was not ready to tell.

Occasionally he would take a mule and go out to the other diggings — to Soames Bar, Cecilville, the colony of Portuguese over on Coffee Creek; and periodically he would go the eighty long miles to Happy Camp. And the word would come back that in all the homes he visited he would leave something holy picture, a crucifix, a charm, something to make the people feel a little more secure in their protection from bad luck or from harm, a little more content with their austere life in the wilderness.

And back home at Sawyer's Bar, he converted the little makeshift graveyard into a cemetery. The funeral services now met with universal approval, and each new grave that took its place in the cemetery had for its marker a beautifully carved block of wood. The lettering was perfect, the angels looked like angels, and even the cameo death's head that appeared on a few of the markers represented the terrors of death with awesome realism. Father Florian's wood carving was indeed a work of art. And some of the more curious, who remembered that strange package he had carried in on his back, wondered whether it might have contained some special tools for this craftsmanship in wood.

Then it came time for the miners of Sawyer's Bar to build Father Florian a church. A suitable place was found at Paradise Flat, on a little rise where it was judged that the gold-bearing gravel had played out.

"After all," said Paddy McGann, who had a hand in picking the place, "it surely wouldn't be the Lord's will to be puttin' the church right on the gold itself. And anyhow, I do be thinkin' of them three dead old pine trees markin' the very center of the place — like the three sorrowful crosses they are, standin' like a sign, as you might say." Father Florian only smiled. And that's where the church was built.

When the day finally came for the first service in that little church on Paradise Flat, the people looked up at the altar. And then they knew Father Florian's secret. There above the altar, hanging as if pinned by a shaft of sunlight from the window and radiating a beauty that had never been seen before in that valley, was an oil painting of the Crucifixion. It was large — five feet wide and nearly seven feet high. This, then, had been the mysterious and wonderful bundle that Father Florian had carried in on his back.

A trained critic might say that it was painted by a skillful artist in imitation of the best 17th and 18th century Austrian painters. He was probably an amateur, but one with great imagination, who must have studied under some trained artist.

The colors were clear, but not bold. The suffering Christ was in the center, with the two other men, dying on their crosses, on either side of him. There were soldiers on horseback, guards gambling for the discarded robes, women in the deepest grief, and the curious spectators in the background — thirty-two faces in all, in a very skillful composition. The horses seemed to move. The faces of the people were shown at various angles, and their expressions were real and very human, from mere curiosity to the profoundest grief. This was certainly a work of art from another world. "By the holy Saints, 'tis a miracle, as you might say," gasped Paddy, and this time he spoke for Sawyer's Bar.

But the greatest wonder of it was the effect the painting produced upon the people who were looking at it. Standing close to it near the altar, they could see the different kinds of sadness, the suffering, the sense of guilt on each face. They felt drawn into the picture to share in the sorrow that they saw there. But as the viewers stepped back down the aisle, further away from the altar, one by one the minor faces faded from sight to become only shadowy background, and only the principal figures remained. And then, as they moved further back, even the more important figures faded away, leaving only the Christ visible. Gone, now, were the faces that showed the grief, the shame, the sense of guilt and sorrow. Only the one figure shone out, the one face remained, and there was no longer to be seen the tension of pain; the suffering was over. In its place there was a glow of triumph. And there arose in all who saw it a feeling of awe before great beauty.

Who painted the picture no one knows. Why Father Florian carried it all the way from Austria to bring it to rest finally at Sawyer's Bar, one can only guess. In 1866, Father Florian left Sawyer's Bar and went to Marysville, where he died in 1868. But this little church still stands, after these hundred years and more, on its high place at Paradise Flat. And if you were to go there today you would find it to be the only part of the old diggings left undisturbed by the great hydraulic stream that later methods of mechanized mining used to cut away the red banks of the Salmon River.

Although the surrounding soil gave up gold dust in good measure, the rocky eminence on which the little church sits remains high and alone and untouched. That little church is closed now, but only thirty-seven miles away at Fort Jones Sacred Heart Catholic Church you can find that mysterious and hauntingly beautiful work of art that was Father Florian's secret.

The Russian and the Lady

It's not easy to tell a love story, especially a tragic one. But when two young people give themselves into the power of love so completely that their whole lives become a sad yet beautiful story, it is not easy to forget them. Their story follows us and haunts us to the end of time. Romeo and Juliet made such a story because their star-crossed love which burned at white heat for so short a time ended in death for both of them. Longfellow's tale of Gabriel and Evangeline was about a long, slow love that burned throughout a lifetime, for the girl, at least, and ended only in death.

There is a love story in Northern California like that, too. The girl was just about Juliet's age, a few months older perhaps. She fell in love almost as fast, and there was an obstacle to her marriage almost as strong as the family objections that drove Juliet to tragic death. But the girl of our story did not die. She lived, like Longfellow's Evangeline, condemned by fate to the stretching years of a lifetime with only the memory of her love. This story has been told many times, yet no one really knows what happened except for a few recorded facts that could be listed on a single page.

The girl had just turned sixteen. She was growing into the full rich beauty of womanhood that only a healthy, happy, well-to-do Spanish girl could be blessed with. She lived with her family at the Presidio of San Francisco overlooking the bay and the narrow straight that was its gateway. The Presidio and the Mission of San Francisco had been established near the pueblo Yerba Buena in 1776, and now after thirty years, life there had settled into a quiet routine that sometimes seemed dull to a sixteen-year-old girl.

Old Governor Jose Arrillaga was like an uncle to her; he often tried to be funny to amuse her, but she had matured beyond his simple humor. Her father was the commandant of the Presidio and was too busy with his affairs to pay much attention to a growing daughter. Her brother was devoting his days to hunting and exploring the region around the bay, and his nights to the romantic adventures so attractive to a young don of such importance. Her mother was busy with the affairs of the home and the servants, but mothers never seem to understand a young girl's loneliness, anyway. So the beautiful Concepcion Arguello felt that the spirited physical happinesss of her childhood was gradually merging into the quiet boredom of decorous maturity. She found herself settling for an uneasy contentment in the daydreams of a young woman.

April 6, in the year 1806, started out to be just another day of quiet routine. But suddenly something happened to change the whole life of Concha Arguello. That morning a strange ship was seen entering the bay. Foreign vessels were not supposed to be allowed in the bay at all. The government had issued strict orders to keep all foreign ships out. But here it came, bold as anything, right up to the little dock that had been built near the Presidio. The shouting from the ship was in a strange language that nobody could understand, and when a few of the men came to land they wore strange clothing that nobody had ever seen there before.

Father Uria came down to meet them because he knew a few words of English, but these big strangers were not English. Father Uria then tried his Latin, and from the little band of strangers an older man with a white beard came forward and said a few Latin words to him. Thus it was, through a faltering conversation that the mystery was gradually unravelled.

The newcomers were Russians. They had come in friendship all the way from a place called Sitka far up the coast to the north. Governor Arrillaga and Concha's father were away at the time. Had they been at home the strangers most certainly would not have been permitted to come ashore, for they were both very strict about enforcing the laws. But in their absence, her brother was the next in authority. He was young and daring, less likely to be bound by regulations from Mexico, and perhaps he was also curious to learn more about these strangers. Possibly, he was a little too proud of his importance to deny himself the grand honor of playing host to these manly beings from another world. At any rate, he extended to the Russians the hospitality of the Arguello home. Concha was proud of him for being so thoughtful and gallant.

That evening at dinner, with the help of Father Uria and his Latin, the story of the Russians unfolded. The bearded man who told the story was a scientist and engineer named Langsdorff. The leader of the party — young, handsome, courteous, quiet, yet very strong looking — was Count Nikolai Petrovich Rezanof, who had been sent to Sitka in 1805 as the Russian government's overseer for the Russian American Fur Company. He had found the community at Sitka threatened with starvation because one of the supply ships from Siberia had failed to arrive. Scurvy had broken out there, causing many deaths, and there was no prospect of finding food in that barren north country. Rezanof had come looking for supplies for his starving village in Russian Alaska. The girl listened and felt sorry for the poor people in the far north, and was glad that they had such a fine young man for a leader. He would save them from starvation if anyone could.

The dinner went pleasantly enough, considering the language difficulty. Count Nikolai smiled and nodded to everyone, but mostly he looked at the girl. Their eyes never met, however, for every time he glanced in her direction the sensitive young lady was gazing down at her plate or her dark eyes were averted in some other direction. She knew, of course, whenever his eyes were upon her. She said nothing, but she listened intently to his earnest talk, so haltingly translated, about the needs of his people.

The evening was a social success. But getting supplies for the Russians of Sitka was not such an easy matter. There was plenty of meat and grain in California, but it was not for sale. It was forbidden by Spanish law to sell supplies to foreigners. A few days later a priest came up from Santa Clara who could speak French, and communication improved considerably.

But communication could not solve the political problem involved. The Spanish were worried about possible invasion by the Americans or the Russians. They could see that they must discourage any attempts by either country to establish outposts or colonies on the west coast. The Russian fur trade was clearly a threat, and it would be very foolish indeed to do anything that would help them hold on in Sitka and eventually expand their operations, which could easily put them in California. The San Francisco commandant knew this all too well, and refused to sell the supplies.

Rezanof, on the other hand, was not the kind of man to fail in his mission. He brought presents to the members of the Arguello family, including magnificent furs for Concha. He began to learn Spanish so he could talk with the comandante and Concha's brother and her mother and of course, with the attractive Concha herself. In the days that followed, the Russian and the little lady of San Francisco saw more and more of each other.

She realized that she was falling in love with this handsome, intelligent, forceful foreigner. Perhaps she had loved him from that first evening. She knew that he had seen the California coast of San Francisco and might even now be planning to establish an outpost nearby. She knew that he was desperate for supplies and would do anything he had to do to get her father and Governor Arrillaga to sell them to him. She knew that he was an experienced man of the world who had probably broken many hearts at the court of the Czar. Yet she also knew that she loved him, and she felt sure that he loved her. Nothing else mattered.

It is possible that Rezanof did fall in love with this eager, young, beautiful, innocent creature. There are those who say that he was only pretending in order to use her help in getting what he wanted. But there are also those who believe that his love was real and the romance which followed was pure and honorable and true. The young couple were properly chaperoned at first, but later as they came to understand each other better they found ways to avoid this old-fashioned convention. They walked alone together, they held hands, they whispered and laughed together, they kissed, they made plans. And in a most honorable way, Nikolai Rezanof asked her parents for the hand of Concepcion Arguello in marriage.

But this could not be. He was a suitable enough young man but for one thing. Their difference in religion stood between them. She was a Spanish Catholic, and he was of the Eastern Orthodox faith. Her parents liked him well enough as a man, but his church, his nationality, his way of life, his purpose in being there were all against him. For the belle of San Francisco, such a marriage would be impossible. But love is stronger than all reason, and finally it was agreed that the young lovers might be married — but only after he had received permission from his church and his Czar to join her faith. Such was the grave decision of her parents. This was a disappointment to the young lovers, who wanted so desperately to be married immediately. But a promise was better than nothing. And so for the next three weeks Concha and her Nikolai were sublimely happy. They dreamed their dreams and counted the thousand joys their future life together would bring.

Meanwhile Rezanof's ship was being filled with the supplies he so badly needed. And on the 21st day of May of that year 1806, he set sail for Sitka. His plan was to go from Sitka to Kamchatka and across Siberia to report to the Czar, get permission for the marriage, and then return to claim his bride, who would be waiting in California. Concha Arguello watched him go, sad at the thought of his long journey and the loneliness of his absence, but she had more than hope for his safe return. She knew of a certainty — her heart told her without doubt — that he would come back. His ship sailed out of the bay and quickly disappeared behind the headland to the north.

Months went by, but there was no word of Nikolai. The time came for his return, and passed, and the weeks dragged into more long months, end on end, yet no news came. Had he reached Sitka safely, or had his ship been wrecked? No one knew. Had he reached the Czar and failed to get permission for the marriage? No one could answer. Had he forgotten her so quickly and turned his attentions to other ladies out in the world? There was no one to answer. But she knew in her heart that he would come back, he must come back. Even through death itself he must surely come back and let her know.

A few years later the Russians established a settlement at Fort Ross, less than a hundred leagues away, but she could get no word from them of Rezanof. It was even rumored that he was there, but no proof could be found. The years slipped by, and still Conception Arguello waited. Each day she looked out at the bay, but no ship came. No other earthly love could ever replace this that had been so true. No other young man dared seek the hand of this woman who lived with her memories. At last she did not look at the bay any more; she no longer prayed for the ship that never came. Finally, gradually, she turned her prayers to other things. Her love was no longer for this earth; she gave herself over to the work of God. She became a nun.

She went to Benicia and helped establish a school there, and her blessed name is still to be found in the diaries of the young ladies who studied with her and felt the inspiring touch of her devotion.

It was not until she had lived with her memories for thirty-five years that she learned the truth. A man named Sir George Simpson came to California in 1841 hoping to buy the abandoned Russian Fort Ross, and it was he who knew the story and told it to the lonely woman. Nikolai Rezanof had indeed reached Sitka. He had kept his word and had gone to Kamchatka. He had started across Siberia to speak to his Czar, but on the journey he became ill. Finally, at a place called Yakutsk, he had died. And through all these years of a woman's waiting, his body had lain in a lonely grave in the frozen earth of northeastern Russia.

And all she had for her years of waiting were the memories of those few short weeks when she was a girl of sixteen, and the certainty now that his love had been true. Her heart had not deceived her. Her Nikolai would have come back to her. But God had touched her life for a greater purpose. Perhaps, after all, her love was purer and richer and more enduring than it otherwise ever could have been.

Hatfield the Rainmaker

The rain had been coming down for a week or more, sometimes in heavy downpours but mostly in a steady, relentless day-and-night soaker. It was the first big storm of the year, and the Santa Rosa Valley in Sonoma County needed it after the long dry summer. The grapes had been picked, the vegetables were all in, the late apples had been pretty much taken care of, and it was now November and time for the change of seasons. With a pleasant blaze in the fireplace, one could settle down to the tranquilizing comfort of a rocking chair and sit by the wide window and look down over the greening foothills to the valley below, now darkened and blurred by the slanting rain.

It was just the kind of afternoon for my old friend Ace Morgan to drop in for a little gab, or play some cribbage, or watch his favorite program — the Lawrence Welk Show — on television and perhaps take Hobson's choice at the dinner table later. He knew he was always welcome, for he had at least two endearing talents: he could spin a good yarn, and he had mastered the not too subtle art of praising my wife's cooking. Moreover, he knew that if he used the right bait and a delicate line he could usually reel in a jar of jam or pickles to take home with him.

"Seems like the rain's early this year, but that's good for the orchards, I guess. Not so good for floods, though. I hear that the Russian River is gettin' pretty high down around Guerneville. Another day of this and she'll go over the banks and make another mess of things. About every year they get flooded out down there, and nothin' much they can do to stop it. I wonder if the PG&E has its rain-makin' machines goin' up north.

"You remember back in '55, or maybe it was January of 1956, when the Yuba River broke loose and just about washed out Yuba City and saturated the whole Sacramento Valley? Well, it was learned later that the PG&E had their rain-makin' machines goin' all the time up in the Sierra and Cascades. That sure didn't help any to cut down on the floods."

Ace settled back in his chair. He was beginning to remember things, and we knew that a story was about to emerge.

"Did you ever hear about the big floods they had down in San Diego back in about 1916? I was there at that time — just a young buck then, but I remember it like it was yesterday. I ought to: I was in water up to the withers, myself. I'll tell you, there's a lot of people down there will remember it. That was a big one. Old Noah himself would have had trouble ridin' that flood to a countdown. But I guess I'm gettin' ahead of myself.

"It was a young feller name of Charley Hatfield started it all. It had been pretty dry around there all through 1915, and by Christmas the whole country was about to burn up. The people couldn't even take a bath because the reservoirs up east of San Diego were empty, and even the jack rabbits had to carry canteens to get from one cactus to another for shade.

"Well, this Hatfield had something of a reputation for being able to make it rain, in some wild and mysterious ways that he called "scientific." He was living in Los Angeles at the time and most people didn't pay much attention to him. But he had made some pretty good claims that he had made it rain in other parts of the country — Los Angeles, Hemet, and even over in the San Joaquin Valley. Fact is, he had made some pretty good money at it. But mostly he just wanted to help people out. I heard tell he came from a good Quaker family with pretty high moral standards, and they weren't out to bamboozle anybody.

"Well, the San Diego city council heard about him, so they called him in. They were desperate! Well, here was Hatfield calling himself a meteorologist with a contraption he said was a moisture accelerator, and he offered to go to work and fill the Morena and Otay reservoirs with rain water if they'd pay him ten thousand dollars.

"By this time the city council was over a barrel for sure, and so they figured ten thousand wasn't too much of a gamble, especially since the deal was that if he didn't fill the reservoirs they didn't have to pay him anything. The whole city council, all but one, voted to take him up on the deal.

"But Hatfield was young and not a very good business man, so they didn't make out a contract — just a handshake agreement.

"Right away he and his brother went out and built a twenty foot tower at Morena. Then they made an eight-foot platform on top of that to put some tubs and other gear on. They built a fence to keep the crowds back, and then they settled down to their scientific work.

"They got a lot of chemicals and mixed them up in some galvanized iron pans and built a fire under the stuff until it smoked and fumed and made an awful stink. Then they put this smokin' concoction on top of the tower and shot it off into the air with rockets of some kind, or maybe it just rose by itself. I don't know. People could see Hatfield smokin' his big cigar and stirrin' up his stuff while his brother kept the fires going, and this went on night and day for nearly a week.

"By the 9th of January it started in to rain, and in a week they had over twelve inches of water in the Morena reservoir. By the 19th of the month, both Morena and Otay were full, where they had never been more than half full before. That rain didn't let up for a minute. Like the feller said, 'It war'nt no little sizzle-sozzle, either; it come a trash mover and a gully washer.'

"When the dams overflowed, folks figured they had had about enough, and they told Hatfield he could turn 'er off now. But she kept on comin' down. I was there and I saw it — water over the dam and people splashin' around everywhere. It did let up for a little while, and then near the end of January here come the rain again, just about as bad as before. Clear over as far as Arizona and up to Los Angeles they never had such a soakin'.

"Then the dams broke, and down she come — a sheet of water headin' straight for San Diego, washin' out houses and barns and livestock as she went. Other floods were happening, too, and the Tia Juana race track got washed out. A big part of San Diego was devastated, and I think about ten or eleven people died, drowned or got lost, on account of it.

"By this time people were yellin' bloody murder on Hatfield and the city council. Charley had to hide out to keep from gettin' lynched. Everybody was ready enough to blame him for causing it all, and some folks started to sue the city for puttin' him up to it. So he had to lay low for a while, but later he went in and asked the city for his money. He had done what he promised; he filled the reservoirs, all right, and then some. But he didn't ask for any bonus — just the ten thousand.

"Now you can see the pickle that the city was in. They had about six million dollars worth of damage claims against them, and if they paid Hatfield off they would be admitting that they

31

were responsible, and people could sue the city to a fare-thee-well. So the city attorney — he was a bright young man named Cosgrove — argued that there had never been a contract. And he was right about that. He also argued that anyway it wasn't Hatfield that brought the rain; it was an act of God. With all those lawsuits against the city, Cosgrove figured that if they could blame God for the damages maybe they could get off the hook. So that's what they did, God being a pretty hard feller to sue, and the city got off easy.

"But this left Hatfield out in the rain all by himself. If he claimed that he was the one that brought the rain, he could probably sue and get his money, or some of it, anyway. But then he would be admitting that he was also responsible for the damage it caused because it was not an act of God but an act of Hatfield. He stood to lose his shirt in damages or get put in jail for all those deaths, or even maybe get himself lynched.

"So there he was with a problem. He acted as his own lawyer, which didn't help him any, and he argued his claim before the city council — even offered to settle for half — but the city chickened out on the deal.

"Hatfield had a few loyal supporters, though, who tried to make a fuss about it, and of course the papers played it up for a while, but then it cooled off and Hatfield drifted away.

"Hatfield did some more rain making in other places after that. Even got forty inches and another flood in the town of Randsburg over in the Mojave desert. But he stayed away from San Diego. He finally ended up, so I am told, in Glendale as a sewing machine salesman.

"For a long time, though, the folks argued over whether he could have done it. They still don't know why some people can find water in the ground with a forked stick, or why some Indians can make it rain by dancin' with snakes. But Hatfield must have been at least partly right, because long after his day the PG&E learned how to make it rain.

"Some folks say that Hatfield always believed he'd made it rain and felt cheated because San Diego never paid him. After all, he didn't tell 'em he could turn it off; just turn it on, which he did. And anyway, Charley Hatfield got to be a real legend in

Southern California, and folks still talk about it whenever it gets awful dry, which is pretty often in that country."

Diamonds in the Big Rock Candy Mountains

The bank stood squarely and solidly on the corner of California Street and Sansome. It was the very embodiment of stability, respectability, and security; and with a president who was none other than the great financial wizard William Ralston, the money-minded population of San Francisco could lie down and sleep, knowing that their money would be safe. Or, as safe as money could be in a year of speculation such as 1871, when fortunes were being made and lost on paper and hard money was changing hands with spectacular rapidity. The public had boundless and unshakable confidence in the bank, the bank had complete and unwavering confidence in Mr. William Ralston, and Ralston had confidence in himself. Everybody who was anybody did business with the Bank of California.

No one was surprised, therefore, when one morning in the summer of that memorable year, two shaggy old prospectors wandered into the bank. They looked at the heavy iron doors, the tall sturdy pillars that stood from floor to ceiling, the black and gold painted iron cages occupied by the tellers, and were obviously impressed. They nudged each other as some stately gentlemen swept past them. Apparently satisfied that the bank was safe and hence merited the confidence of men of substance, they approached a teller and, with some hesitation and awkwardness, they produced a rough buckskin bag which they placed gently on the counter.

"I reckon you got a good strong safe here, young fella," said one of the prospectors.

The teller answered, "Yes, of course."

"Well, we can't tote this thing around with us, and we'd take it right kindly if you'd lock it up for us for a few days," said the speaker, while his companion nodded vigorously and patted the buckskin bag with loving gentleness.

"Yes, I can put it in the safe. But first I must record the contents. What's in the bag?"

"Well, now, we didn't figure that would be none of your particular business. No offense meant, of course," answered the spokesman of the pair.

"It's the bank's rule," explained the teller.

The two men looked at each other as if to estimate the importance of this unexpected development.

Apparently assured by his companion's slight nod, the older man mumbled, "Well, I guess it's all right. They's just some diamonds and things like that."

The teller's ears pricked up and his eyebrows arched a little as he took up the bag, hefted it, set it to one side, and wrote the receipt. As the two prospectors pocketed the piece of paper and strolled out, the teller made a quick mental note of their names — Philip Arnold and John Slack. The unusual nature of the transaction aroused his curiosity, and as he went to put the bag in the safe he couldn't resist the temptation to peek inside, fully confident that the old man had been lying. He untied the bag and took a furtive squint. Then he looked again. Sure enough, the bag was full of sparkling stones — diamonds and other gems. Such a discovery was too important for the teller to keep to himself, so he went back to the inner recesses of the bank and knocked on the door of President Ralston to apprise him of the matter.

The strange story provoked his curiosity as well, so he came out and also looked into the bag. He thrust his hand in and brought out — lo and behold! — a handful of diamonds. The gems were indeed an eye full, but Ralston guessed that there was more here than met the eye. Inquiry revealed that both Slack and Arnold were known around San Francisco as part-time prospectors with good enough reputations, so Ralston sent a messenger to find them and bring them back to the bank.

"Boys, where did you get these stones?" he wanted to know.

"Well now, Mr. Ralston," said Arnold, "you know how us prospectors are. We just don't rightly know. We ain't surveyors. Off to the east there in the hills, mebby a thousand miles, but we ain't tellin' just where. Leastwise, not exactly. You shore understand that, Mr. Ralston, sir." And Arnold swept his arm off toward the east that might have indicated Nevada, Wyoming, Utah, or Arizona. Ralston offered to buy into the proposition, but the old boys reckoned that they didn't want to sell. They were perfectly satisfied to live off the diamonds and leave well enough alone.

But finally, after much consultation they let Ralston persuade them to sell him a small interest in their diamond mine, about $100,000 worth. They did happen to need a little ready cash, so maybe a little partnership wouldn't hurt. Ralston lost no time in drafting an agreement and advancing them the money.

Now that he had bought a percentage of the mine, the banker was entitled to see the source of these fabulous stones, or at least have his representative inspect the diamond field for him. That seemed fair enough, so a Ralston man was selected to go with the prospectors to their secret Ophir to confirm its reality. They boarded the train and went to Rawlings Springs, Wyoming. There, as they stood on the railroad platform and looked out toward the hills beyond, the prospectors announced their determination to enforce one of the conditions of the deal; the city man would have to be blindfolded when they got close to the diamond field. Men who discover a mine are very canny about letting every Tom, Dick, and Harry know where it is located.

They rented horses and set out from Rawlings Springs, and for three or four days they rode through the rough country. Every once in awhile Arnold or Slack would climb a hill, look around to get his bearings, and away they would go again through the brush, across rivers, and always up and down hills. After about five days of this, the time came for the Ralston man to be blindfolded. Another day and a half, and they reached their destination, a rugged bedrock country somewhere in the wildest part of Wyoming or northeastern Utah. Here at last was the fabulous diamond field. And it was real. They found diamonds. The precious gems were lying around almost on the surface of the ground where apparently they had weathered out into sight. To the young representative's amazement, as they searched for samples, they found more than diamonds; a few sapphires and rubies also turned up. But mostly it was diamonds.

When they returned with a few samples as evidence, the city man happily reported that there was indeed a diamond field, and right away Mr. Ralston got excited. Or as excited as a sophisticated banker can allow himself to get when he has almost within his grasp the treasures of Aladdin, Midas, and the Count of Monte Cristo all combined. He had a friend, Asbury

Harpending, who was working on some high finance in London at the time, and Ralston sent him a long telegram describing the discovery. That telegram cost him $1,100, but the message was worth millions.

At first, Harpending thought he was crazy and didn't pay much attention, but message after message went to London and finally Harpending confided the matter to the Baron Rothschild, who was perhaps Europe's greatest financial genius of that day. Rothschild knew that strange things had happened in America. As early as 1866 real diamonds of commercial value had been discovered in Butte County, California. So it was indeed possible, and he became interested.

Harpending came back to the United States right away, and since he was to be allowed in on the deal, he demanded more samples. So Arnold and Slack were sent out again with instructions to bring back about a million dollars worth of specimens. The astute financiers were determined to get more than enough security before they turned loose any big money, and the reluctant prospectors agreed. After a few weeks they returned with a sack of the gems. They said they had had two sacks but had been caught in a flood and lost most of the samples. But then, what's a half million dollars worth of diamonds when a world's fortune could be picked up so easily? Harpending eagerly took the sack to his home, and Ralston and a few other carefully selected and privileged friends gathered around — diamonds, rubies, sapphires, and even a few emeralds. Here was a treasure that would be a bigger bonanza than the Comstock lode, worth more than all the diamonds in South Africa.

The next day the gems were placed on display in the bank's window for the envious public to marvel at. A few people started to rush off to the diamond fields; but since no one knew just where to go, some went to Arizona, others to Colorado, and still others just went looking. Wild rumors spread, and the excitement increased. This might be bigger than the gold rush back in '49. But the bankers knew how to conceal their eagerness. They said, "We won't put out any more money until we make sure. Let's have these stones appraised by Tiffany of New York."

So off to New York and Tiffany's went the bankers, the speculators, and the old prospectors. The latter went along just for the ride, to see the sights and enjoy the fringe benefits of the trip. At Tiffany's the great jeweler himself examined the stones and pronounced them genuine. Then he sent a sample off to his lapidary for a more specific analysis. He warned them it might take a couple of days for the lapidary to make an accurate appraisal, but that was all right with the Westerners.

Meanwhile the story leaked out, and the aging Horace Greeley came around to investigate; so did General George McClellan and a few other important people. When the report came back from the lapidary it was that the raw gems were genuine and probably of great value. Now the financial wizards made ready to swing into action.

First a little legal business had to be attended to. Since the mining laws of the United States had not taken into consideration such things as diamonds, Ralston had to get some of his lobbyists to put a bill through Congress expanding the mining laws to include precious stones and the processing of them. The plan now was to organize a company and cut their own diamonds on the west coast. This, of course, would draw the diamond cutting industry from Holland, a shocking prospect that caused great concern throughout the world.

Speculators little and big clamored to get in on this tremendous deal, but no investors were to be allowed yet. The bankers were holding back to make sure. They engaged a geological engineer, a great expert on mines by the name of Henry Janin, to examine the precious diamond field himself and make the final analysis of the property. Arnold and Slack were not sure they liked the idea of having so many people go out and see that claim. A fellow has to protect his property, and they didn't want any strangers in on the discovery; after all, they hadn't wanted to sell in the first place. Reluctantly, and after much persuasion, they consented to accept $600,000 for a two-thirds share of the enterprise, and on these terms they were willing to show Janin their claim.

After due preparation a small party, including Janin, got on the train and away they all went back to Rawlings Springs. Once again they headed for the diamond field. As before, the trip took several days. At one point along the way someone thought he heard a train whistle, but it was passed over as being too impossible to believe.

Finally they came to a plateau about 7,000 feet elevation and covering an area of some forty miles. This was the place. The experts began to dig around and, as before, diamonds and other precious stones came up. Some of the tiny pieces were even found in anthills.

The geologists examined everything carefully and pronounced the discovery genuine. With this joyous news the company in San Francisco sprang to life. They incorporated for ten million dollars. With the announcement that they would cut and polish in California, the diamond industry of Amsterdam shuddered in helpless horror, and the stock market quivered. If it proved out that diamonds could be so easily obtained, and in such great quantities, the whole diamond industry of South Africa would be ruined, and that in turn would shake the financial structure of Great Britain and all of Europe. But Harpending and Ralston were equal to the challenge. Only the closest friends of the bankers were permitted to buy in on this multi-million-dollar enterprise; small investors should not be allowed to take such risks.

The next spring, while the entrepreneurs were dreaming of their great financial revolution, a young government geologist named Clarence King heard about the diamonds and became suspicious. He warned Ralston that something didn't seem quite right, but the banker was too deeply committed by now to pay any attention to the young man. King thought he knew just about where the field was from the information that leaked out, so he decided to see if he could locate and examine it. Quietly he and a German diamond expert set out to investigate for themselves. Arnold and Slack suddenly became restless and demanded the balance of their money, which Ralston by now was willing to pay, and the old men pocketed their profits and dropped out of sight.

King found the plateau. He even found diamonds. On examining an anthill the German friend said, "My, these ants are very accommodating; they are mining the diamonds for us." He picked up one of the tiny stones, examined it carefully through his glass, and exclaimed, "Why, they even polish them for us!" One of the stones indeed showed the marks of the lapidary. They now had proof that the diamonds had been "salted" in the field. In fact, it was later said that the "planting" had been a little too promiscuous; they even found diamonds in the forks of trees.

A telegram went out immediately from King to Ralston informing him of the hoax, but by then it was too late; Arnold and Slack had disappeared with their booty, and the company was worthless.

If you look at it right, this is a good example of prospector's luck. Lady fortune remained faithful to those old boys all the way. Any good geologist should have known that rubies and diamonds are never found together in the same formation, and certainly not in the crevices of sandstone or in tree trunks. The Tiffany appraisal was incorrect, but that is because Tiffany dealt only in cut stones and hadn't much experience with raw diamonds. As for the train whistle, that was real. With all their winding around the hills and through the rivers, they were never more than a few short miles from the railroad that brought them.

Where did these low grade diamonds come from? Some say the prospectors had secret backers. But Arnold had made a stake of $50,000 or more in a mining deal with which he made several trips to London and Amsterdam and bought a supply of cheap uncut stones. He sprinkled in a few good raw diamonds of high quality in order to make the appraisal come out right. His profit on the investment was considerable.

As soon as Ralston knew he had been bamboozled, he started paying off his debts. Ashamed because the hoax had stemmed from his own greed, he wrote the necessary checks so his friends would not suffer too much for his stupidity. The old prospectors — well, it turned out they were cousins, both from Kentucky. Arnold went back home and with his share bought a fine estate. He also bought a bank. Slack disappeared for a while — some thought he was killed for his money — but eventually he also turned up in Kentucky and went into the undertaking business.

Some of Ralston's partners later went to Kentucky and tried to sue Arnold, hoping to get some of their money back; but as the story goes, Arnold had a lot of friends and relatives down there who met them at the county line with shotguns and explained that Kentucky wasn't healthy for Californians at that time of year. So nobody touched Mr. Arnold and Mr. Slack and they enjoyed the fruits of their labors. In fact, they became something of heroes in that part of the country. And William Ralston, when his cancelled checks came back, framed them and hung them on his office wall as a reminder of the $600,000 joke he had played on himself.

Now, this is only one version of the story. Some historians say it didn't happen this way at all. They say that Arnold was a pretty smooth mining man well known in San Francisco and Arizona, and not a grizzled old prospector at all; that there were others in on the deal who persuaded Ralston that the diamond field was real; that the salted mine was in Colorado, Arizona, or somewhere else; that it was not Tiffany's but a San Francisco jeweler who appraised the gems, and that different amounts of money changed hands. But in any case this was one of the biggest swindles ever to hit these parts.

Black Bart, Shotgun Poet

The stage pulled out of Fort Ross on time. It was the pleasant morning of August 3, 1877, and the driver felt good. So did the Wells Fargo guard who slumped beside him on the high driver's seat. There were no passengers this time to worry about, and with a light coach the driver felt like hitting a good fast clip; perhaps they could reach Guerneville a little ahead of time for their evening stop.

The road was rough and the curves sharp, but the coach bobbed along, sometimes squeezed between steep hills covered with tall brown grass, and sometimes free on the open headlands in close view of the ocean. As they approached the wide barren space where the Russian River emptied into the Pacific, the road swung eastward and followed the winding river past Duncan's Mills.

Ahead was a sharp curve in the road. The river came up close on one side, and on the other was a huge rock jutting out from a heavy thicket of brush on the steep hillside. As the horses trotted around the curve they suddenly shied. There, standing squarely in the road, was a strange apparition that waved a shotgun up and down and yelled, "Halt!"

The driver instinctively kicked on the brake, and the coach came to an abrupt stop. Taken completely by surprise, and in consternation at the unbelievable sight before him, the Wells Fargo guard only opened his mouth and stared. "Well, I'll be damned," he mumbled under his breath.

The figure in the road stood forked-end down like a man, but the top part was a white flour sack with a black hat on top of it. It also had arms that held a shotgun which meant business clearly enough, and so did the two eyes that glared through holes cut in the flour sack under the hat.

"Will you please throw down your box — and also the express mail sack?' came a hollow, almost mournful voice from the flour sack. The two men on the coach looked at each other, then complied without a word. The heavy box' hit the ground and rolled over; the mail sack plopped beside it. "Thank you kindly, gentlemen," said the hollow voice. And then to the uncomfortable guard it added, "You must have been asleep. You should be more alert."

The guard squirmed. "Well, I guess my weather eye wasn't peeled this time, and that's a fact."

The figure in the sack examined the coach and found it empty. "I must apologize, gentlemen, for the delay. Now you may drive on."

The driver promptly shook the reins, and the stage moved off down the road. As soon as he dared, the driver looked back, and there, standing in the middle of the road, was the frightful figure actually waving goodbye to them.

They made it to Guerneville on time, reported the robbery, and the local constable and his deputy rode out to investigate. When they returned to the crowd waiting for them in the Gueneville saloon they had something strange to report. There was no doubt the robbery had taken place just as the men had described. They had found the place where the mail sack and box had been dragged off the road. The sack had been cut open and the mail had been rifled for valuable contents. The lock on the Wells Fargo box had been pried off and the money taken. But the box wasn't empty.

In the box on the back of a way-bill, written in a fairly neat hand, was a little poem which read:

> I've labored long and hard for bread,
> For honor and for riches —
> But on my corns too long you've tread,
> You fine-haired sons of bitches.

It was signed, "Black Bart the P-o-8." And below the poem a little note was added: "Driver, give my respects to our friend, the other driver; but I really had a notion to hang my old disguise hat on his weather eye. Respectfully, B. B."

This was the first professional job of Black Bart the P-o-8. He had taken about $300 in cash from the Wells Fargo box, a check for $305.53, and a few dollars from the express mail. Hardly good wages for such an artistic effort, but this was only a beginning, a sort of dress rehearsal you might say.

There were many strangers in Guerneville that night, all interested in details of the robbery. The poetry was passed around and read and re-read, much to the amusement of all. One man in particular seemed to be especially interested in the story, an inconspicuous little man with a thick mustache and gray chin whiskers, wearing the average traveling man's neat clothes and talking with the average traveling man's customary friendliness and good humor.

It was nearly a year before the flour sack struck again. This time, July 25, 1878, it was the stage between Quincy and Oroville that was robbed. The lone bandit, with his shotgun and white sack, got a little more for this effort; the cash box contained $379, and from a generous passenger came a $200 diamond ring and a silver watch worth about $25. This time our baleful bard left another poem which contained the previous verse left at Duncan's Mills a year before and two additional verses that went like this:

> Here I lay me down to sleep
> To wait the coming morrow —
> Perhaps success, perhaps defeat
> And everlasting sorrow.
> Let come what will, I'll try it on,
> My condition can't be worse;
> And if there's money in that box,
> 'Tis money in my purse.

And it, too, was signed, "Black Bart the P-o-8."

The following October he showed up again. This time his mark was the stage running between Covelo and Ukiah on the Willits grade. There was a dangerous bend around which the stage had to go just before reaching an underpass. The rock stood up on one side like a big black thumb, and the surrounding area was full of buckeye brush and poison oak. Black Bart set up five dummies in this brush — shirts, pants, and hats realistically stuffed with straw — placed strategically so they could be seen vaguely from the road. Some of those accomplices held guns that Bart had stolen in Willits.

As the stage went around the rock towards the underpass, Bart rushed out in front of it, waved it to a stop, and yelled back to the stuffed shirts in the bushes, "Wait, boys. Don't shoot!" His dummies obeyed. Then Bart had the driver throw down the cash box and drive on. He dragged the box behind a hill and broke it open only to find nothing inside. Local folklore maintains that later when the box was found there was a note inside which read,

> "Here I stood in the snow a-sobbin'
> and a-waitin' for a stage not worth a-robbin'."

This note was posted in the deputy sheriff's office in Ukiah, where it remained for a long time.

In the six years of his career Black Bart gained a much greater reputation than he deserved, and his robbin' profits were low. Shaggy bits of doggerel began to appear at the scenes of other holdups that he obviously could not have committed. Genius generates imitation, and in Black Bart's case his modus operandi, complete with flour sack, derby hat, and poetry, was popular among less inventive highwaymen for many years. It is ironic and perhaps even poetic justice that the real author of the following apocryphal lines will never be known:

> This is my way to get money and bread;
> When I have a chance, why should I refuse it?
> I'll not need either when I'm dead,
> And I only tax those who are able to lose it.

> So blame me not for what I've done,
> And I don't deserve your curses.
> And if for some cause I must be hung,
> Let it be for my verses.

Bad luck finally caught up with Black Bart on November 3, 1883, when he attempted to rob the Sonora-to-Stockton stage near Copperopolis. How this happened was vividly recalled by Mrs. Sanelli of Columbia years later when she was 105 years old. She remembered that the bandit came to her mother's boarding house the night before the robbery and asked for a room. There was nothing about him to attract suspicion. He was a well-dressed gentleman, cordial, quite ordinary, and no one paid much attention to him. The next morning he departed. And that same morning her fifteen-year-old brother, Jimmie Rollerie, decided to go to the hills and try out a new rifle. He was hunting rabbits in the brush some distance from town. On reaching a steep hill, he decided to come out of the brush and walk along the road for a while.

When he reached the top of the hill he saw, down the other side, that the stage had been stopped. A man with a sack over his head and a shotgun in his hands had ordered the driver to unhitch the horses and proceed on up the hill toward where Jimmie was standing. The boy immediately knew what was happening, and as the driver reached the top of the hill Jimmie shot at the robber, who was tugging at the money box. He dropped the box and ran into the brush holding his wrist, and Jimmie was sure he had scored a hit.

The Wells Fargo detective, J. B. Hume, was not long in coming to the scene of the robbery. At the place where the bandit had waited for the stage and to which he had fled after the unsuccessful attempt, they found several clues, the most rewarding being a discarded handkerchief that bore a laundry mark FXO7. This was the first time in six years that detective Hume had found anything he could go on, and of course he immediately began to search for a laundry that could identify the mark. Finally, in San Francisco, he found it; the laundry had given that mark to a man named Charles E. Bolton, who lived at the Webb House on Second Street, San Francisco.

His real name was Charles E. Boles. He was a dapper, middle-aged man who sported a cane, wore a diamond tie pin, was a smooth talker with a sense of humor and, after he was caught, willingly discussed the hold-ups. As a consequence, he went to San Quentin, where he resided for the next five years. The story is told that when he was leaving prison the warden said, "Well, Charley, are you going straight now?"

Boles, alias Bolton, answered, "Yes, Warden, I shall never commit another crime." Then the warden asked him whether he intended to write any more poetry, to which he said, "I've just told you, Warden, I promise to commit no more crimes."

After 1888 Black Bart faded from sight, and it is presumed he went back east to his family. There were numerous stage robberies for which he was blamed, but they always turned out to be imitations. It has been said — and it could be true, though there is no proof of it — that Wells Fargo made a deal and paid him $206 a month not to rob their stages. He disappeared, but like most folk characters, he did not die. He has passed into the everlasting history of the West for his shotgun, his flour sack, and his so-called poetry.

He is remembered as a fine gentleman. He never killed or even hurt anyone. His shotgun was never loaded. He always worked alone, except for the dummies that occasionally backed him up. And he robbed only Wells Fargo. He never robbed the U.S. mail because, it was said, he didn't want to get in trouble with the Federal Government.

And in Guerneville the older residents will still point to a spot in the hills where a little cabin once stood that they called Black Bart's cabin. He is supposed to have stayed there that night in 1877 when the stage was robbed near Duncan's Mills, this dapper little man with the thick mustache who got so much pleasure out of the public reading of a poem by Black Bart the P-o-8.

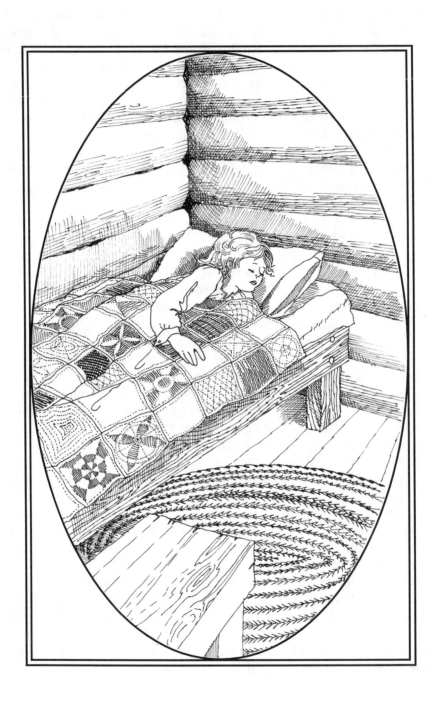

Once Upon A Winter Night

The winter of 1860 was a "closed" winter. The weather was bad all over, but in Northern California it was worse than anywhere else — and in Fall River Valley, all the way from the Pit River to Goose Lake, it seemed to be the worst of all. The snows came early that year and piled deeper and deeper, so the deer that normally came down out of the high mountains to feed through the winter on the juniper, oak, and bushes in the valleys found themselves unable to push through the heavy drifts and were beginning to perish. The small herds of cattle in the foothills were pinned down by the snow, and the few scattered ranchers who had stayed with their spreads in the outer regions of the valley were not able to reach their cattle, either to take them food or even to bring in the hides and meat from their emaciated bodies when they died of cold and starvation.

When the snows finally stopped, a blue cold settled over the valley; all forms of life there grew numb, and nothing moved. A ranch five miles away was as far off and as impossible to reach as if it were over in Nevada. The Turner cabin was only fifteen miles from Fort Crook, but it might as well have been a hundred miles, as far as Tom and Maggie Turner were concerned.

As the days wore on into December, the meat supply began to give out, and finally they were down to one small front quarter of venison hanging in the little lean-to shed by the back door — that and a little flour left in the bottom of the sack that lay crumpled in the big box under the cupboard near the kitchen stove. Maggie had watched the flour in that sack grow lower and lower, and her concern had gradually increased to quiet alarm, but she said nothing. No need to set her man to worrying; it wasn't his fault. And Tom, each time he had cut a slice from that quarter of meat, had privately resolved to eat a little less each day. He and Maggie might go hungry, but the child would need all he could get.

Tom and Maggie had named their son Little Sperry, after her brother, but somehow Little Sperry T (the T was for Turner) had got itself shortened to "Little Sport," and the name fit him. He had been an outdoor child, a very active boy — that is, until the sickness got at him. First the pains had hit both of his legs, but later had seemed to settle in one leg, and it was beginning to look as if he couldn't move it any more the way he ought to. And then that fever had come to eat up his strength.

"I just don't know what to do," Maggie had said one night after Little Sport had put in a particularly painful day. "It ain't like anything you can doctor for."

"I been thinkin'," Tom had said, more to himself than in answer to Maggie, "that them Injuns might could of had something to do with this."

"Why, Tom, I thought them Injuns was right friendly to him. Seemed like they was, anyhow." Maggie believed that she had a feeling about people that reached beyond the understanding of her husband.

The Indians in question were a small band of Achumawi — maybe twelve or fifteen, more like a big family than a band — that had come into the foothills near the Turner place to pitch their little camp where a spring came out of the lava outcroppings. Little Sport had gone over to investigate one day and had stayed to play with the Indian children. In fact, by pine-nut gathering time, he had set up quite a friendship with the Indians, so much so that Tom had muttered his displeasure several times, but Maggie had always put it out of his mind. That was before the winter had set in and Little Sport had been taken down with the fever.

"I ought to a-turned them scurvy devils in and got rid of 'em." Tom's conviction was growing that they were somehow responsible for his son's condition. He could easily have turned them in, as he put it, to the soldiers without incurring any disfavor either among the ranchers of the valley or the government. First the Pit River Rangers and then General Kibbe and his "Guards" had been over at Fort Crook rounding up the Indians of Fall River Valley and packing them off to a reservation somewhere.

The Rangers and the Guards were ruthless in their treatment of the almost defenseless natives who were armed only with bows and arrows against the white man's guns. Most of the Indians had been wantonly killed as they tried to escape the wrath of the white men, running like frightened rabbits through the brush. Those that had surrendered had been herded together, and the ones that could walk the long journey were taken to a reservation over on the Mendocino Coast. The few that had escaped to the hills were gradually drifting back into the valley as they felt it was safe to return. Such were the little group that had settled near the Turner place. Timid at first, they had gradually gained confidence and even a feeling of security when they realized that Tom Turner was not about to betray them to the Rangers.

This little group didn't seem to be up to any mischief against him, so he never found it very urgent that he take a hand against them. Besides, come spring, if they survived the winter, they might even be able to do some work for him around the place. A little cheap help would come in handy. Several other ranchers had used Indians to good advantage, and he might as well give it a try also.

But now he was thinking about Little Sport. The boy shouldn't have got in so thick with those Indians. They had curious ways with their medicine, and they could have put a curse on the child or fed him some kind of poison. But now, there wasn't much need to do anything about it anyway; they couldn't possibly survive this winter. If they had been foolish enough to stay camped in that draw between the rough ridges of lava; they would starve out or freeze out, and that would be that.

The wind was rising. It was a cold night wind blowing out of the north, and more storm clouds were gathering. The little cabin seemed almost to hunch closer to the ground and brace itself against the black, cutting cold. The fine dry snow, driven by the wind, found cracks between the logs and under the rafters and came sifting in. There was plenty of wood for a warm fire in the cookstove, though, and as the night packed down around them; Tom and Maggie sat closer to the stove. The sick boy lay on the bed in the corner, turning and whimpering in his sleep, and Maggie went over to make sure that the big patchwork quilt was tucked in over his shoulders.

"Won't be able to get out again tomorrow," Tom said. "Be no deer where I could get at 'em anyway. I was hopin', though, to get some fresh meat for dinner, tomorrow being Christmas and all."

And Maggie said, "I've still got a little sweetenin' on hand, and I was figurin' to make some kind of taffy for Sperry. Seems like he ought to have a little something for his Christmas, even if he can't rightly enjoy it."

"That'd be real nice." Tom almost smiled at the thought.

"The boy had something on his mind about Christmas," Maggie went on, as if she hadn't heard Tom. "Seems like he had something fixed up with that Injun boy — the one that's just about his age. He said he had been talking with that boy about what Christmas was supposed to mean, and I think he had his heart set on giving some kind of present to that Injun. Seems like he kinda wanted to get them Injuns to believing in Christmas, too."

"Well, it won't make no matter now, I reckon. They're prob'ly all froze dead, anyway."

51

The wind howled outside like a living thing, like a wailing animal trying to push inside. And then suddenly there came another sound. Something truly alive was outside the door. There was a fumbling at the latch. Tom reached over to the wall and picked up the rifle that was leaning there. Slowly the door swung in, and a figure stood hunched in the doorway. It moved a step or two inside, and little ringlets of snow fell from its feet and etched its footprints on the floor. It was an Indian.

Tom's finger felt for the trigger of his rifle. The Indian's eyes darted around the room, as if searching every corner. Then with one hand raised, palm forward, he quickly backed to the door, closed it, and leaned a little against it. His moccasins were worn almost through, his buckskin leggings were torn, and his shirt was ragged. Over his shoulders was a loosely sewed rabbit skin robe, which he clutched together in front at his waist.

"Now look here, Injun!" Tom demanded. "What do you mean, bustin' in here like this?"

"Me come friend," the Indian said, and his eyes turned toward the figure of the little boy lying on the bed.

"Well, I guess you can come in and warm up," said Maggie, who noticed that the Indian was trembling. He came quickly toward the fire. As he reached out his hands to warm them, Maggie thought she noticed a spot or two of dried blood on them. But maybe it was only patches of dirt. The rabbit skin robe fell loose, and the jagged hole in one side of his shirt showed bigger. It looked a little discolored, as if blood had hardened there.

Tom saw it too. "Looks like you been hurt in the flank, there. What happened to you?"

"White man shoot. Long time ago." But they could see that the old wound in his side was still tender. Tom leaned his gun back against the wall. The Indian turned and looked a long time at the dishes still on the table from the meager supper that the couple had eaten earlier.

"Well, I do believe this feller's about famished," said Maggie.

"He can warm up, and that's all. We ain't runnin' no hotel," said Tom.

"Seems just like he might a-been 'sent' here," said Maggie, who sometimes felt that her sixth sense was a little more acute than most people's — or maybe it just worked out that way sometimes. "I've heard of things like that, just to try people for their goodness."

"He ain't been 'sent,' and he ain't here as a 'trial' to us. He's here for what he can get, you can bet on that. Where you from, Injun?"

"Come long way away." The Indian looked again at the boy on the bed. "Boy catch-em sick, mebby?"

"Yeah. Boy catch-em sick." Tom grunted. But Maggie was still thinking.

"I don't remember this one from them Injuns over by the spring." And without another word she went to the shed by the back door and cut off a piece of meat from the quarter of venison hanging there. She put it on the stove to fry, and set about getting some bread from the cupboard. Tom watched but said nothing. The Indian watched, also in silence. When the food was finally set before the dark stranger, he bolted at it hungrily as if it were the first food he had tasted in days. Every morsel was cleaned up before he relaxed his eating. Then, with a short grunt, he moved over to the bed where the boy lay. Tom again reached for his gun, and Maggie put her hand to her heart — not so much in fear as excitement.

The stranger bent over the sick boy and touched his forehead, his cheek, his stomach, and one leg which lay as only a vague outline under the thick quilts. Then, turning to the anxious parents, the Indian said simply, "He will be good again." And from somewhere hidden under his shirt he brought out a pair of child's moccasins. They had been worn but were still beautiful in their workmanship. The stranger gently laid them inside the crooked arm of the sleeping boy and stepped back. "Indian boy, all same him brother. He make present. All good."

The visitor then moved toward the door as if to take his leave. Tom cleared his throat, and the stranger stopped.

"Say, them Injuns over by the spring — them people there — are they all right?" he asked. And then, with a little self-consciousness, "I was just a-wonderin'."

"Alive, yes," the Indian answered. "But heap hungry. No got gun; no can kill deer. Must all die, mebby."

Tom was about to say something else, but Maggie had already burst into action. She hauled out the flour sack and poured at least half of the little that remained there into another sack. Then she quickly went to the back door and returned with the thin shoulder of venison and sliced off half of it lengthwise of the bone. This she wrapped in a clean dishrag and put it in the sack with the flour.

53

Quickly, as if not daring to pause or think, she thrust it at the Indian.

"You go and give them folks this stuff. It ain't much, but it might tide 'em over. We got a gun and can get more meat when this weather breaks." The Indian took the gift without a word and passed through the door. Tom and Maggie followed him to the door and looked out after him. Something strange had happened. The wind had ceased. The storm clouds were gone. The snow lay still and white, glistening in the moonlight, and a few stars sparkled in the quiet sky. The Indian was nowhere to be seen. It was as if he had vanished without leaving even a footprint in the smooth blanket of snow.

"I reckon I'll be able to hunt tomorrow," Tom said.

"We ain't a-going to miss that meat and flour," Maggie said, as she went to put the sack away. "Seems to me that flour sack is just about as heavy as it was before — maybe heavier, for all I can tell."

"Looks like you didn't cut off much meat, either. Can't hardly tell where any is gone. Anyway, I'll have some fresh meat for dinner tomorrow." And then, as if in answer to her unasked question, "Well, I guess I just feel lucky, that's all."

"I'm a-thinkin' more'n that," Maggie answered. I'm a-thinkin' that tomorrow, being Christmas, our boy is going to put them moccasins on. An' he's a-goin' to walk, too. I feel it in my bones."

And the stars shone down that night on the little cabin, and time glided over into Christmas.

The Dream and the Curse
of Sam Brannan

Many a man has had a noble dream on which he has ridden to great heights of glory. But there is also such a thing as a great curse that can draw a man down from the top of the world and wither his soul and destroy his mind and body. Anyone doubting this can consider how this happened to one of the noblest Californians of them all, Sam Brannan of San Francisco and Calistoga.

Sam Brannan was a magnificent man. In the first place he was an Irishman. He was not very tall, but was broadshouldered, handsome, and "a fine figure of a man," his friends said. He had flashing eyes and a broad, friendly smile. His courage was boundless and so was his generosity. With such qualities to support his ambition, Sam Brannan became California's first millionaire. He helped organize the first school in California and the first newspaper in San Francisco. He also started the vigilantes to combat crime in that lawless young city. And it was Sam Brannan who, in a special way, started the great gold rush to California. Yet a curse followed him to the highest pinnacle of his success, and it dogged him down to the bitterest depths of failure, despair, and death.

Before he came to California from New York, Sam Brannan was a follower of Joseph Smith and a member of the Church of Jesus Christ of Latter-Day Saints. In other words, he was a Mormon. After Smith's death and when Brigham Young was planning to move his people across the United States to pioneer a new land that was then part of Mexico, Sam Brannan played his part by chartering a ship, *The Brooklyn,* to bring a party of Mormon colonists — over two hundred of them — to California. They made the long voyage around Cape Horn, then out to the Sandwich Islands, and finally in the summer of 1846 they sailed into the bay at Yerba Buena.

Churchman though he was, Brannan had never been a spiritual man; on the contrary, he was very worldly, and he saw his big chance in this new place. But he was also a Mormon leader, so in the spring of 1847 he went back eastward over the Sierra, across the Nevada deserts, to meet Brigham Young in the Salt Lake Valley, where he tried to persuade Brigham to bring his Saints on to California, a rich and fertile land where they could prosper. But Brigham Young and his people stayed in their Deseret, a territory which had its center in the valley of the Great Salt Lake.

Brannan came back to California disappointed and bitter. He continued, however, as head of the Church group in California, to act as the religious as well as the temporal leader of his little colony, and he regularly collected the tithing of his Saints. They faithfully paid him their Church dues, one-tenth of their earnings, and he put the money away. Some said he was using it to finance his own projects, but whether he spent it or saved it, one thing is sure; he did not turn it over to Brigham Young and the Church as he was expected to do. Finally, the Church needed the money, and Brigham sent two apostles to collect it. They were accompanied by Young's avenging angel, the zealous, long-haired, gun-carrying Porter Rockwell. They asked for the money, and Brannan simply said, "No."

"It's the Lord's money, and Brother Brigham wants it," pleaded the Church representatives.

"If it's the Lord's money, let the Lord come and collect it. I'm not giving it to Brigham Young."

The cold-eyed killer, Porter Rockwell, reached for his gun, but Sam Brannan stood his ground. The apostles said, "We're here to collect it in the name of the Lord. We'll give you a receipt for it."

"If the Lord wants it," snorted Brannan, "let the Lord give me a receipt for it. I'm not giving it to you." Angry words flew back and forth, but Rockwell did not shoot, the apostles did not get the money, and apparently the Lord did not come forward with a signed receipt. Brannan kept the money. But soon afterward, another apostle, Parley P. Pratt, came with the authority to impose extreme punishment on the stubborn Mormon; he pronounced official excommunication, which cut Brannan off from the Church and condemned him to eternal damnation. In the confrontation which preceded the excommunication, Apostle Pratt reached the end of his patience and cried out in rage, "You are a corrupt and wicked man, Sam Brannan. You are a thief. You shall be cast out of the Church. You shall die in agony and poverty and grief, without a dime to buy a crust of bread!" That was the curse that burned itself into the memory and through the soul of Sam Brannan.

But these were good times in California, and Sam Brannan continued to prosper. He became a rich and successful merchant. He started his newspaper, *The California Star,* and made it pay. He bought land in Yerba Buena, later to be called San Francisco, and he acquired property in the Sacramento Valley. In 1848 gold was discovered at Sutter's mill. The word leaked out, and one of the San Francisco newspapers printed a brief story on it, but it did not attract much attention and Sam's editor said he doubted that it was true. "I don't know," Sam Said. "This is a great country. It could be true. I'll go up to Sacramento and find out about it."

So he went to see Sutter and learned that it was indeed true. With canny forethought Sam bought up all the available supplies and tools that miners would need, stocked his store in Sacramento and set prices for a high profit. Then in order to make the news dramatic enough to excite the people, he rode frantically through the streets of San Francisco shouting, "Gold! Gold on the American River!" This is what started the stampede. Within a few days there was scarcely a man left in San Francisco. Everybody was out in the hills and along the rivers looking for gold with supplies purchased from Sam Brannan's store at a tremendous profit to him.

During the frantic years that followed, thousands of adventurers poured into California. San Francisco became a cross-section of the world. Besides native Indians and Mexicans, there were people from all the states — Orientals, Sandwich Islanders, South Americans, Europeans, Australians — all kinds of men from everywhere. A gang of ex-convicts from Australia settled in the city and became organized as a criminal underworld. Another gang of hoodlums, who posed as patriots to justify their lawlessness, were called the "Hounds" because they wanted to hound out all foreigners. This pack of cutthroats robbed, murdered, burned, and looted for profit. Obviously, something drastic had to be done.

To help crush these lawless elements, Sam Brannan organized the Vigilantes, a group of citizens who took the law into their own hands because the law was too weak to protect them. If they could not have law, at least they could have order. These were Sam Brannan's days of triumph.

But he went on to even more wealth and power. At one time he owned about one-fifth of San Francisco, one-fourth of Sacramento, and a large ranch near Yuba City. Yet something was beginning to work against him. Perhaps it was Parley Pratt's curse. His wife, Eliza, grew dissatisfied and squandered his money. She hated his coarse manners and the rough companions that Sam associated with. She yearned for the fine society of New York and the elegant manners of Europe. Finally she persuaded Sam to go to Europe on a grand tour, but his heart was in California. Everywhere he went he bought things to send back home. He shipped some fine merino sheep to his ranch near Yuba City and sent home special citrus fruits, shrubs, and trees of all kinds, including mulberries for an experiment in raising silk worms.

In 1859 he went into the northern part of the Napa Valley and there he discovered something new — geysers and hot springs surrounded by fine land. He remembered the spas and health resorts he had visited in Europe and decided that here would be an ideal place to establish a resort of his own. With the natural hot water, he could build baths, and it would become a place of recreation for the wealthy and the elite, like Saratoga Springs in New York.

Sam bought a large tract of land, erected a splendid hotel, and put in luxurious baths at the hot springs. He built a stable and stocked it with race horses. He planted vineyards and started a winery, planning to make good wine and brandy to be shipped east. And to get people to his resort, he even built a railroad. All of this cost money, and by 1860 he had put all he had into the project. For the great occasion — opening his fabulous Saratoga of the West — he gave a big banquet at his hotel for all his friends. Even the fabulous Lola Montez sat at his side, and Sam Brannan was exultant. The champagne was plentiful and everyone drank freely. When the time came for him to make his speech about this wonderful place which was to be the Saratoga of California, Sam rose, flushed with champagne and happiness and his tongue was thick. He waved his arms and shouted, "And we'll name it the Calistoga of Sarafornia!" And that's the way the folk in the Napa Valley explain the naming of that fine old town that Sam Brannan once owned.

But the place did not make money. His wife divorced him and took all the property she could get. His children turned against him, and he grieved over the loss of his family. All his investments were going bad, many of his friends were deserting him, and by now he was drinking too much. The curse of Parley Pratt was working.

Finally, Sam Brannan had to give up his Calistoga dream, but he did not stop looking for new lands to conquer. He turned to Mexico, put his remaining money into the cause of the patriot Juarez, who was fighting to overthrow Maximilian, and hoped eventually to gain a profit from Mexican lands and bonds. He got involved in a colonizing scheme in Mexico and for a while things looked good — on paper. He even married a beautiful Mexican girl and apparently she made him happy. But the land development failed and Sam lost his money. His lovely Mexican wife, who was faithful to him as long as he had promise of wealth and power, eventually left Sam and went back to her people. His failures drove him to uncontrolled drinking, and that led to dissipation, degradation, and poverty.

But there was always the dream. Sam returned to Escondido in Southern California, and there he made another desperate effort to regain his fortune. With a little money he had recovered from Mexico, he went into real estate. Out of this venture he got only enough money to finance a trip to San Francisco to pay off such old creditors as he might find; and he even left his nephew enough money to pay his funeral expenses, for Sam Brannan was sick and he knew he was going to die.

He sailed to Southern California again, returning to his little boarding house in Escondido. (He brought with him as a present to the old woman who looked after him, just a pair of gloves and a bottle of perfume.) He was seriously sick now, and almost immediately after his return home, he had an attack. It was said he had an "inflammation," but what it was exactly we don't know. His landlady put him to bed, making him as comfortable as she could. Later that night, after washing the dishes, she went to his room, turned on the little music box that sat on the window sill, and as it tinkled the "Londonderry Air" she sat by the bed to comfort him.

Sam's mind was beginning to wander. He took her hand and looking as if into space, he said, "Listen ... I am Sam Brannan ... I am rich ... I've made millions. Parley Pratt said I'd die without a dime, but I've got him there." He reached for his old pants and fumbled in a pocket. With a trembling hand he took out the last money he had in the world, a twenty-dollar gold piece. He held it up and cried, "I've fooled him!' and somehow he got the idea that the old landlady was his beautiful Mexican wife. "I've got money in my hand and my good wife by my side." The music box tinkled on, and death came to Sam Brannan.

The people still say that the curse had burned his soul. Sam Brannan, who had been California's first millionaire, died in misery and poverty almost alone. Sam Brannan, who had enjoyed the love of many women including the beautiful Lola Montez, died holding the hand of an old boarding house woman who scarcely knew him. The man who had loved California so much and had been like a raging torrent in her early stream of history, settled into death like a drop of rain lost in the ocean. For many years even his lonely grave lay forgotten and neglected. Now only the legend remains.

The Spirit of Joaquin

In a little cabin on the Stanislaus River in central California lived a young Mexican. He was a very handsome young man, Joaquin, apparently of a good family, who had come up from Sonora, Mexico, to farm and perhaps pan a little gold in this new land of El Dorado. With him was his lovely young bride, Rosita. Or perhaps her name was Carmelita; the stories differ, and no one is quite sure. And also with the young couple was Joaquin's brother.

Together, in that little cabin by the river, they lived through a quiet, happy summer. They took a little gold from the stream, and they talked about how they would plant some corn when spring came. They knew nothing of the Californian's laws, and when it was explained to them that it was illegal for Mexicans to own mining claims or take gold from the California rivers, they merely shrugged and went on with their work. God had put the gold there. It belonged to everybody. And they took only the little that fortune put into their hands to pay for their work.

The Californians were angry about this, and one night a small group of men, drunk on liquor and mad with hatred, burst into the cabin on the river. Angry words ensued, then threats, and a fight! Joaquin's brother was shot down immediately. And Joaquin's beautiful wife — innocent, frightened, helpless — was brutally attacked and then murdered. Joaquin fought like a madman, but he was outnumbered. The Californians tied him to a post out in the yard, stripped him to the waist, and with a horsewhip lashed him until the blood came. As he stood there straining at the ropes, each time the leather whip cut across his bare chest and shoulders, he swore an awful vengeance. He memorized the ugly faces of his attackers and swore that he would kill them every one, and all the other Americans that he could. Then he slumped into unconsciousness, and his assailants left him for dead.

We are told that the next day Joaquin disappeared, that he drifted north after that, but no one knows for sure where he went. The marks of the whiplash gradually healed, but the memory of his pain and the hatred for his enemies seemed to grow stronger. The next time he appeared it was as a bandit. As an outlaw he gathered around him a band of other Mexicans who had grievances, and he took in some who wanted a quick profit and were not afraid to kill for it. Soon the handsome young Mexican became the powerful leader of bold and ruthless outlaws. Always splendidly dressed, he rode at the head of his band on a magnificent horse, and his very name struck fear to any who might stand in his way. The men who had killed his wife and brother one by one disappeared, and everyone knew what had happened to them.

He was a cruel and deadly enemy of his foes, but he was never known to turn down a friend who needed help. Many poor Mexicans received his generous help, and they thanked him and asked the saints to bless him. Whenever he needed a place to hide, they sheltered him and kept his secrets. He had become their Robin Hood.

In 1851 Joaquin and his gang settled about three miles north of Marysville. They stole horses, robbed immigrant wagons, held up stage coaches, and killed whomever got in their way or were so foolish as to try to capture them. The vigilantes organized a large force to hunt him down, so Joaquin quietly slipped away and went further north and wintered near Mount Shasta. After that, he was always on the move. At San Jose a posse almost cornered him, but he got away. Some say he went to Carmel Mission, and it is said that a priest at the mission painted his picture.

There was such a picture, and perhaps it was painted by a priest. It shows a man supposed to be named Joaquin, with wild eyes, a fierce moustache, and a cruel face. Other artists later copied this picture — or some other — and in each successive portrait the outlaw became more dashing, more handsome, more gallant, and his costume became more colorful and splendid. These pictures only reflected the growing legend.

There is a telling of how a cattle buyer was camped by a little stream one night as he was driving his cattle to market in one of the San Joaquin Valley towns. Five young Mexicans rode into his camp just at dusk and asked for some supper. He obligingly gave them food, and they spread out their bedrolls and slept by his camp that night. The next morning, when they awoke, he was cooking breakfast for them.

"Well, how is Señor Joaquin this morning?" he asked.

The young leader looked startled and suddenly became tense. One of his companions drew his gun, looked a long time at the cattleman, and then grinned. "So you theenk you know heem?"

"Yes, I knew him the minute he rode in last night," said the cattleman. The Mexican then asked why the driver hadn't killed him while he slept at night, to collect the reward.

"Why, that's easy, friend. I don't like to kill men. And I don't want the reward. Besides, you fellers never did me any harm. If every man that deserved to hang went supperless, there'd be empty chairs at more tables than mine," said the cattleman. Joaquin smiled and promised the man that he would never be sorry. And the people say that from that day on, this man never lost a head of cattle to any Mexican bandits.

The reward for the outlaw Joaquin grew. It attracted many adventurers, some of whom gave their lives to the vengeance of Joaquin. With increasing interest and satisfaction, he read the reward notices. One beautiful Sunday morning in Stockton, while the bells were ringing for church and the fine ladies and gentlemen were walking to worship, a handsome young Mexican came riding along the street on a beautiful black horse. He was wearing a fashionable sombrero, flashing buckles, and spurs of silver. He stopped here and there to look in the shop windows. The young ladies cast admiring glances his way and thought, "What a rich young man he must be."

He rode over to the side of the building where some posters had been nailed to the wall. One of the posters read: "Reward: $5,000 for the bandit Joaquin." The stranger got off his horse, took a pencil out of his pocket and wrote something over the poster. Then he remounted his horse and rode away. The ladies and gentlemen rushed up to look at the poster to see what he had written. On the reward notice he had crossed out the $5,000 and had written under it, "I will give $10,000," and it was signed, "Joaquin."

This romantic bandit was said to be the kind of man who couldn't live long without love, and there were many beautiful ladies willing to share his company. One in particular was a fiery beauty called Antonia la Molinera. She ran away with him, dressed like a man, and rode with him in the hills. She fought beside him on his raids, and it was said that they were happy for a time. But after a while Antonia fell in love with another member of Joaquin's gang, and one night she slipped away with him and they disappeared.

Once again Joaquin swore vengeance, and no one doubted would keep his vow. For months he followed the lovers' trail from village to village and from ranch to ranch. At last Joaquin found the man and killed him. The girl knew her turn would surely come, that she would never be safe until Joaquin was caught; so, secretly, Antonia sent word to the man who was most likely to capture the bandit, and she told him where Joaquin's hideouts were.

That man was Captain Harry Love, a hunter of men and an adventurer who had come up from Texas. He yearned for the excitement of the hunt and hungered for the reward money that stood on Murieta's head. The state legislature authorized Captain Love to organize a posse of rangers to track down the outlaws. The state paid them $150 a month and the rangers furnished their own horses and outfits.

The orders were to get Joaquin and as many of his gang as possible, and particularly a wanton killer known as Three-Fingered Jack, who was riding with him at the time. Love had learned from the treacherous Antonia where Joaquin's hide-out camps were located, and the long hunt began. The rangers chased the bandits from one camp to another, night and day, through the hills, across the rivers, and over the mountains, gradually closing the circle. Finally, early one morning in July, 1853, the rangers came upon the last camp. They were in the mountains near Tejon Pass in the Tehachapis. They rode quietly up over a ridge and suddenly, there below them, was a little camp hidden in a pocket in the rugged canyon. Six Mexicans were seated around the fire. Breakfast was being prepared, and some were already eating. A seventh man — slender, graceful, with dark eyes and long black hair — was standing a little way from the campfire rubbing down a beautiful bay horse. This was Joaquin Murieta.

The rangers rode in quickly with their guns drawn and ordered the bandits to surrender. For a brief moment there was silence. No one moved. No one spoke. Joaquin's guns were hanging on his saddle several feet away from where he was standing, just out of reach. Three-Fingered Jack stood back against a rock, watching every move. He was tense and ready. Suddenly Joaquin made a dive for his guns. This was the move that sprung the action. Three-Fingered Jack whipped out his guns and began to fire. A burst of gunfire came from the other Mexicans, but their shots went wild. Love and his rangers dug spurs and lunged into the camp, firing at Jack. Their lead hit him again and again. He slumped, fell, and was dead.

Joaquin couldn't quite reach his guns without moving directly into their fire. So he leaped on his horse, and without saddle or bridle, the horse bounded away over the hill and up among the rocks. Through the brush and over the hills he flew, with the rangers after him. Joaquin had no gun, only a dagger which he brandished in the air as he pushed the horse on. The rangers were following, shooting as fast as they could. At one precipice, where the rocks hung low overhead, Murieta was scraped off his horse, but he leaped on again and away they went.

Finally, one bullet found flesh, and the horse fell. Joaquin was now on foot. He scrambled among the rocks and behind the bushes. The shots were still coming. Three bullets entered his body, and he began to fall. He sank first to his knees, then to his elbows, and finally he lay in the sand. Then he raised one hand as if to stop the shooting and said, "It is enough. The work is done." And Joaquin Murieta fell dead. The long trail had ended.

The outlaws' lair in the mountains was too far away to carry the dead bodies in from, so Love and his party cut off the head of Murieta and the hand of Three-Fingered Jack to deliver as proof that they had killed the bandits and thus collect the reward. Preserved in alcohol, these frightful objects were accepted as evidence that the outlaws were dead, and on August 18, 1853, the head was placed on exhibition in San Francisco. The curious were thus enabled to see what was left of the man who but a little while before had been a living legend, Joaquin Murieta, the Robin Hood of El Dorado. For this great privilege it was necessary only to pay the small admission price of one dollar.

It took only three short years to create the legend, and it still lives today. The name of Joaquin is seen everywhere in the great valleys of California, and the people say that the spirit of Joaquin still rides the California hills. Even a grizzled old poet of the Sierra, Joaquin Miller, took the outlaw's name and wrote a poem about him.

The legend will not die. And wherever unjust laws or greedy men oppress the poor, some Joaquin Murieta or another Robin Hood will ride again.

The Siege of Sebastopol

"Well, now, I want to tell you them Russians had just ought to be taught a lesson. Why, they just move into a country and take over with their tyrannical methods, and it's high time they was stopped."

"... Tin't none of your business, Jeff Stevens, nor mine, nor this country's. A body'd think you was just tryin' to egg this country into a war with Russia the way you talk."

"No I ain't looking to make no war. But it seems to me that if you was a real patriotic American you'd be ashamed to stand by and watch them despots walk all over people. They've got a big army and some mighty smart engineers, and if they ain't stopped right where they are they'll be tryin' to take over the whole of Europe before you know it. That's what I think, Charlie, like it or not."

This conversation was taking place in the little community of Pine Grove in California, not far from the Russian River, in the year 1855. The British, French, and Italians were at war with the Russians, not in Europe but in Turkey, in the Crimea. The Black Sea, Sebastopol, and Balaclava were being talked about as far away as California, and the military bungling of the British was being watched and deplored day after day as the newspapers brought reports from the fighting front.

It was August, and fall was in the air. The fog that rolled in almost every night from the ocean a few miles away stayed later in the morning, but the crispness of the early hours always melted into the mellow warmth of mid-day. Loafers could still spend afternoons sitting on the pants-polished wooden bench on the shady side of the country store. Soon they would have to move inside the store or over to the livery stable, but for now it was pleasant enough just sitting and arguing over events of the day, both domestic and foreign.

Jim Daugherty's store was a social necessity in Pine Grove. The gentlemen of London might have their clubs and the financiers of New York or San Francisco might have their card rooms, but the aristocracy of Pine Grove had Daugherty's store. From 1849 to 1854 it had been Miller and Walker's store and post office combined, and it had served its mainfold purpose steadfastly and well. It supplied the hauled-in groceries and food stuff to feed the inner man, it provided ready-made clothing to warm and adorn the outer man, and it afforded the social environment essential to stimulate the thinking man. The post office and Postmaster J. N. Miller served all the little settlements for the coast and the lower Russian River and therefore attracted a steady procession of visitors from the back country, which was considered somewhat less civilized but not to be ignored because of its abundance of fish and game and other earthly resources.

So when a man named Morris bought the store and moved it to his own lot in another section of Pine Grove, its clientele moved with it. And when in 1855 Daugherty bought it and moved it again, the whittlers' bench went along without question. The Pine Grove boys considered the store nothing less than an institution of learning; and in winter, the cracker barrel by the stove or in summer, the old bench outside, were the institution's fraternity house and debating platform combined.

In 1853 the French and English fleets were in the Dardanelles as a gesture of strength intended to frighten Czar Nicholas and his Russians, who had moved forces into Turkey. It was Jeff Stevens' considered opinion that the Russians were there to force the Russian Orthodox religion on the good Christians of the Roman persuasion, and that having achieved a religious monopoly in the Middle East they would proceed to take over politically. Hibbs, on the other hand, argued that it didn't matter much; there weren't many Christians in Turkey, anyway. Joe Morris, who had once owned the store and had named the community of Pine Grove and therefore lent considerable prestige and weight to the discussion, pronounced the resounding judgment that even if the French and the Russians wanted to fight each other, the British would never go to war.

In 1854 England allied with France and declared war on Russia. After more than a year of wrangling, the contending political factions had decided to fight, but there was considerable doubt as to what they were to fight for, and there seemed to be no good place to do the fighting. Finally the Crimea was selected as a likely spot to strike at the Russians, whose fleets dominated the Black Sea. And so in September the English and French armies arrived in force before the Russian naval base at Sebastopol and laid siege to it.

In America, the abolitionist movement was growing. In Pine Grove the argument gravitated sometimes to slavery here at home, and sometimes to the Crimean war, depending on the tone of the most recent news dispatches from San Francisco, which was the center of the outside world.

So that's how it was on this August afternoon in 1855. Joe Morris opened the debate with the opinion that England ought to be just about ready any day now to crush the Russian resistance at Sebastopol and take the city. Charlie Hibbs cocked his head knowingly and said, "Now, you shore are whistlin' up a holler tree, sayin' that. You know dang well that them English ain't showed nothin' but fool stupidity ever since the dang thing started. Why, if I had a tomcat couldn't fight better'n that, I'd skin him out and give him away for fiddle strings."

And as usual when Hibbs spoke, Jeff Stevens took up arms in the opposite camp. "They're just a-takin' their time, that's all."

"Yea, they're takin' their time, all right. And that's all they're takin'. Been just about a whole year tryin' to get them Russians out of Sebastopol, and nothin' come of it. Wouldn't surprise me none if Queen Victory herself would have to go over there and take a broomstick to 'em; her dang armies can't do it."

"You don't know nothin' about them armies. Look what they done at that other place last year — Balaclava, wasn't it?"

"Well, what did they do but get licked?"

But Stevens wasn't ready to give up his point. "The way them English fought in that battle, they was pretty hot mustard, I'd say. You ought to read it the way it was wrote up by that Lord Tennyson. They made a charge that must have been somethin' to behold."

"I read that piece. Cannon to the right of 'em, cannon to the left of 'em, and when it was over there wasn't enough left of 'em to take home for mincemeat."

"What's the matter with you, Charlie Hibb? You talk like you was soft on them Russians. You ain't got sympathies tied up inside that city of Sebastopol, have you? Hey, fellers, maybe Charlie's got a old girl friend in there with them Russians and he don't want the English to break in on 'em."

"No, I ain't got sympathies," said Charlie. "All I got is the sense I was born with, that's all."

"Meanin' I ain't?"

"Meanin' you ain't."

"Now hold on, there," said Jeff Stevens, turning a little red around the ears. "When you start throwin' personal insults, you're drivin' nails a little too close to the quick. I ain't a-goin' to stand for it." And Stevens began to lose his temper. The more he talked, the angrier he became. And Charlie Hibbs didn't help any. He responded in kind, and the controversy was no longer a matter of international war; it became highly personal, and what started as banter quickly became insult.

69

In Pine Grove, as indeed in any self-respecting town in the far west, there was only one outcome once a personal offense had been committed against the good name of a gentleman. There had to be a fight. The fact that Jeff Stevens was a big man, over 200 pounds, and Charlie Hibbs was not much more than a runt made little difference. Jeff delivered Charlie a blow in the chest that knocked him sprawling. As Charlie scrambled to his feet, Jeff had picked up a substantial stick, one that old Captain Auser had brought along as a walking cane, and he made for Charlie brandishing the stick high in the air.

Retreat was the only move left for Charlie Hibbs. He grabbed the porch post and swung himself over the railing of the front step and darted into the store. Jim Daugherty, who was standing in the door of his store watching the affair, stepped back and held the door open for Hibbs. When Stevens reached the door Daugherty blocked his way.

"Now, will you just hold your horses there one minute," said Daugherty. "Ye'll not be fightin' no brawl in my place this day. Go along with ye' and get a glass of beer and cool off."

Stevens was about to leave when Hibbs poked his head out under Daugherty's arm. "And if you come back, bring the British army with you," he taunted, and ducked back into the store. Infuriated, Stevens rushed the door again, but Daugherty held him off.

By this time a crowd had gathered. The philosophers of the whittling bench were joined by several curious neighbors and a few strangers from out of town. Encouraged by their presence, Jeff Stevens converted his onslaught into a siege.

"If you wasn't such a coward, you'd come out here and fight," he yelled. For reply, a dried onion came hurtling through the door toward him. Jeff ducked, and in so doing he picked up a rock. The store door slammed shut and the rock bounced harmlessly off the porch.

"You come out here. Sooner or later you got to come out, and when you do I'll be waitin' right here. If you ain't a Russian, then that store ain't no Sebastopol. So remember, I'm waitin' for you."

But the store had indeed become the Sebastopol for Charlie Hibbs. For the rest of the afternoon he hid out in there, while Jeff Stevens waited outside. As evening wore on, Jeff began to feel other drives than that of revenge. A great thirst came upon him, but he was saved from perishing by a generous cheering section who provided him with a glass of beer. Then a great hunger reminded him that his siege of Hibbs's Sebastopol had lasted beyond dinner time. Finally, with a great show of frustrated heroism, he gave up the blockade and went away, with most of the crowd following him.

After that, Jim Daugherty's store in Pine Grove had a new name. It became known far and wide as Hibbs' Sebastopol. In September of that year the real Sebastopol in the Crimea on the shores of the Black Sea surrendered. Czar Nicholas had died, and for the English there was little glory in the victory. The peace was as uncertain as the war had been, and the world turned its interest to other things. People soon forgot about the Turkish city of Sebastopol that had withstood a siege of almost a year.

But in California this other Sebastopol that had once been Jim Daugherty's store in Pine Grove was not forgotten. And since the store and post office was the favorite meeting place for the people of western Sonoma County for a long time after 1855, it is not surprising that whenever a person or a piece of mail was directed to the Sebastopol of Pine Grove it always got to the right place.

So it came to pass that when the town was finally laid out and its legal name was bestowed upon it, Pine Grove faded from existence and out of memory. The town was officially named Sebastopol, the name it still bears. The name has nothing to do with the Turks or with the Russians who came to California and settled at Bodega, Fort Ross, and the Russian River in the early days. It has only to do with a fight that took place in Jim Daugherty's store between Charlie Hibbs and Jeff Stevens, and it is Stevens himself who must bear the responsibility of picking the name.

Lola Montez and Lotta Crabtree

"My grandfather stood out in the rain one night for two hours just waiting to see Lotta Crabtree come out the back door of the theatre. He handed her a little bunch of flowers, and that was it. Didn't even speak to her. But he was in love with her." So spoke an elderly dowager of Pasadena and a patron of the theatre one day as we were reminiscing about some of the early day actors and actresses of the West and the marks they had left on our culture and history. "And my great-grandfather, if I had known him," she continued with a suggestive twinkle in her eye, "might have had something romantic to tell about Lola Montez. She was quite a sensation in her day."

The names of these two fabulous women, Lola Montez and Lotta Crabtree, are linked with the history and folklore of Northern California. Their paths crossed here, and they knew and influenced each other, though ever so slightly, in the town of Grass Valley in 1853. They were like two people passing each other on a mountain trail, pausing for a moment and then going on, one upward to success, fame, and fortune, and the other downward to failure disappointment, poverty, sickness, and death.

When the Forty-Niners came into a mountain region to search for gold, the first thing they did was set up their diggings and go to work. But they also needed recreation and entertainment, so it seemed quite appropriate for them to establish the institutions needed to support their taste for gambling, liquor, dancing, and other pastimes. There was a natural scarcity of women in most of the mining camps, and the few females of the species who did inhabit such places found themselves almost worshipped like goddesses.

Grass Valley was just such a lively camp in the 1850s, and it was here that the beautiful and notorious Lola Montez came in 1853. She brought with her a husband — her most recent one — Patrick Hull, a newspaperman of San Francisco who had become enslaved by her charms. The enchanting lady was also known as the Countess of Landsfield, a title that had been bestowed on her by the infatuated King of Bavaria. Lola was born Eliza Gilbert of Limerick, Ireland. She was a very beautiful girl, and at the age of eighteen she was romantic, ripe, and ready for picking. Her mother, a scheming woman, saw great matrimonial possibilities for such a beauty and arranged a marriage between the girl and an eighty-year-old rich man. But young Eliza had better ideas than to throw herself away on an old man like that, so instead she threw herself away on a young army officer with whom she eloped and went off to India, leaving her mother and the wealthy old man to console each other as best they might.

That elopement started a long series of romantic escapades that gave Lola a great variety of experience and a shady reputation. Eventually she went to France where she became active in the salon of George Sand the novelist and where she became intimately acquainted with Franz Liszt and Alexandre Dumas. At the height of her career she was the "toast of Europe" and almost toppled the crown of Bavaria when the King himself fell madly in love with her. But complications resulted and the scandal forced her to leave Europe. At last, after triumphant conquests of New York, New Orleans, and other big American cities, she arrived in San Francisco. She came as an actress. Although she was publicized as an actress, singer, and dancer, achieving great popularity among those eager to see this notorious beauty, as a matter of fact her dancing was mediocre, her singing was bad, and her acting was worse.

Naturally, her great popularity without talent gave rise to all manner of criticism and parodies. In San Francisco she came up against one Dr. Robinson, who was a producer of plays and a clever writer. Because of Lola's undeserved acclaim, he began to write satires poking fun at this fabulous woman who was making a great deal of money from people of no taste who came to see a celebrity with no talent.

A real actress in San Francisco, Carolyn Chapman, played parts that satirized Lola. On one occasion Lola had acted three parts in a play, so the next week Miss Chapman opened in a show called "Actress of All Work" in which she played seven parts. Then Dr. Robinson, capitalizing on Lola's sullied background, wrote a play called "Who's Got the Countess?" This set all San Francisco to laughing. The ridicule was more than Lola could take, so she left the city and went to Grass Valley, presumably for a year of rest.

In Grass Valley she set up a salon, smoked her Spanish cigars, and invited young people in to discuss problems of the day, sing the latest songs, drink the best wines, and read the latest plays. It was like the grand days in France when she was part of the artist colony of George Sand. Obviously, she was well known in the community almost immediately, though it took the more respectable ladies of Grass Valley some time to accept her.

It was said that Lola was very fond of all animals, bears in particular; she owned two tame bears, kept them on silver chains, pampered them as pets, and even played with them. On one occasion one of her bears, growing too large to handle and getting a little too playful, put his arms about Lola and embraced her a little too energetically. Lola was afraid she might lose a rib or two in this demonstration of affection, so she screamed for help and the neighbors rushed in to save her. After rescuing the lady and taking the bear away in disgrace, the miners decided that it had committed a felony or at least a misdemeanor. So they dragged the poor creature across the street for a lynching. Fortunately, cooler heads prevailed, and they decided to give the bear a fair trial first and do the hanging later. A judge was chosen and a jury selected. One man acted as prosecutor, another volunteered to be the bear's defense attorney, and they tried the bear for attacking Lola. The jury finally brought in its verdict, and the bear was acquitted. The foreman of the jury explained that the bear had acted under due provocation and that anyone under similar circumstances would have embraced the beautiful lady in a similar way.

Lola was particularly fond of children, and the boys and girls going to and from school would often stop in her yard. She was generous to all human creatures in need and made many missions of mercy out into the nearby mining camps. She also went to the camps to entertain the miners with her famous spider dance, which never failed to please. Pinned to her rather scanty costume she had India rubber spiders that would wiggle and jump as she whirled and twisted in her dance, which was a vague imitation of the Italian tarantella. But she was not of a temperament that could remain long in one place, nor could she keep her great popularity. After a couple of years in Grass Valley, she drifted away to other lesser adventures. She was by now on her way down, both as an entertainer and as a beautiful enchantress.

By this time the stage was set and the audience ready for a new theatrical sensation. That new actress was to be Lotta Crabtree. Little Lotta was born in 1847 in New York. In 1852 her mother brought her to California to find her old man, Mr. Crabtree, who earlier had come west to seek his fortune, but he had not been doing very well. They finally located him in Grass Valley, probably because that was where Mr. Crabtree found the "bars" more enticing. It was there that little Lotta came in contact with Lola Montez, who saw in her a girl with talent. She taught the child to dance "The Sailor's Hornpipe" and other simple steps and to sing a few comic songs.

One day when Lola was out riding, with Lotta accompanying her, they stopped in Rough and Ready, another mining town nearby. As the story goes, the blacksmith there, pounding on his anvil while making horseshoes, boasted to the loafers in his shop that he could hammer out a tune by striking different parts of the anvil. Hearing this, Lola lifted the little six-year-old Lotta Crabtree up on the anvil and there for the spectators she performed one of her dances. She so pleased her audience that Lola knew immediately here was a potential actress and she offered to teach the girl all she could, promote her, take her to the cities, and put her on the stage. But Mother Crabtree thought otherwise. The time had come for them to get down to the serious business of earning a living, Mr. Crabtree's habits being what they were, and so the family moved to Rabbit Creek, which is now La Porte, and there they set up a boarding house.

They were making a meager living at the boarding house when the same Dr. Robinson who had lampooned Lola Montez in San Francisco came through with a show. He had a child act, a little girl who could sing and dance for the miners. A man named Mark Taylor ran a saloon in Rabbit Creek, and Robinson tried to make a deal with him to present the show on his premises. They could not agree on terms, so Robinson set up across the street. Immediately, Taylor called in Mary Ann Crabtree and together they fixed up a costume, a little Irish outfit, for Lotta, and brought the moppet in to put on a show in competition with the talent from the city.

The result was destined. Little Lotta stole the show and all of Dr. Robinson's audience, too. This is what started Lotta Crabtree and her mother on their career in the entertainment world. They got some mules and set off to tour the mining camps. Old Papa Crabtree could not be found when they left, so they cooked a pot of beans and left it on the stove for him, scrawled a farewell note, and away they went to Bidwell Bar, Rich Bar, Quincy, and around the circle of northern camps, finally ending in Oroville. The girl sang, danced, and put on a little act, and at the end of each performance the miners would shower her with gold. They would throw gold nuggets, sacks of gold dust, gold and silver watches — just about anything of value, including a few gold teeth. If she could not pick it all up and hold it in her hands, she would take off her slipper and fill it with the gifts in such a charming way that this became part of the act.

From Oroville they worked their way up the Sacramento River and over the mountain to Weaverville. There it was discovered that the Crabtrees were going to have an addition to the family, so Mother Crabtree stayed in Weaverville and sent Taylor, who was managing the enterprise, to San Francisco to get on with his managing; Lotta she sent to Eureka to stay with friends for the winter. Then in the spring they got back together again in San Francisco, which became the headquarters from where they went out to the various small towns and mining camps.

One of their tours included the town of Sonoma, where they put on a show that proved to be the beginning of one of Lotta's favorite and most successful acts. She was a vivacious, redheaded girl who could easily make an audience laugh. At Sonoma she came onto the improvised stage, looked at the audience, and giggled. The act was in pantomime; she did not say a word. She giggled some more. Then the giggle became a real laugh. Then more laughter, louder and heartier. Something was growing more funny by the second, and soon the audience was laughing with her. Finally she had the entire crowd rocking with laughter. No one knew why, but the whole thing was very funny. The climax was wild laughter and thunderous applause, the little girl had her delighted audience in love with her.

Throughout her career she was a jolly comedienne with dancing eyes and a sparkling personality that followed her through her whole life. She learned to play the banjo and sang minstrel songs. She went to Virginia City for awhile and then to Oregon, where she got into a little trouble because she insisted on singing songs from the South. This was fine when she was a little girl; but now she was growing up, the Civil War was coming, and anti-Rebel feelings were running high. She was hissed by some of the Northern sympathizers there, but undaunted, she went off to New York and climbed slowly but surely to fame and fortune as a great entertainer.

To all external appearances, Lotta seemed happier than she really was. No one could get very close to the young actress; her possessive mother, for whom the young star had become a valuable property, chaperoned her completely and drove away all male admirers. She permitted Lotta to have no close friends, no private life, and absolutely no romantic interests. They worked hard, made their money, and saved it. As a result, Lotta Crabtree became both successful and wealthy. Near the end of her career she began to give her money away.

At one time Lotta felt the urge to do something for one of the churches back East, so in Europe she had a beautiful stained glass window made that cost $20,000 — much more when the shipping charges were included. She offered it to the church, but in those days it was not strictly moral for any upright person, and particularly a church, to accept a gift from an actress, for everybody knew that all actresses were sinful. Consequently, the beautiful stained glass window stayed in its crate for forty-two years. After Lotta's death the estate advertised the window to anyone who wanted it. By then people had become a little more broad-minded, and an Episcopalian priest from a poor parish in the Middle West said he would like to have it for his church.

He acquired the window, very carefully uncrated it, got one glimpse of its inspiring composition and indescribable beauty — and then the whole thing collapsed. He spent years after that putting the window back together again piece by piece, and we like to imagine that it is finally in its proper place shedding its holy light over an appreciative congregation.

When Lotta died, still unmarried, she was worth over four million dollars, which was a tremendous fortune in her day. She left her mark in many places and in diverse ways. She donated a fountain to San Francisco, and in her will she left all her money to charities of one sort or another, including shelters for animals, aid for veterans, and funds for the rehabilitation of criminals.

The Old West was more romantic because of these two famous ladies and the legends that have lived after them — one, Lotta Crabtree, who was on her way up to fame and fortune and the other, Lola Montez, who was on her way down. Lola lived only a few short years after she left Grass Valley, and not much is known of what she did. The notice of her death in New York is eloquent in its direct simplicity: "Eliza Gilbert — died January 17, 1861. Aged 42 years — widow. Born in Limerick, Ireland. Place of death — 194 West 17th Street. Cause of death — pneumonia. Undertaker, Isaac H. Brown. Deceased also known as Lola Montez." There was scarcely enough money left in her estate to bury her.

A Mountain that was Named by Fate

She stood on top of the mountain and filled her lungs with the cool refreshing air. A few tiny clouds almost level with her eyes floated over the valley to the south, dotting its green floor with moving shadows. She looked westward, where the hills and forests broke along an irregular line that marked the rugged edge of the Pacific Ocean, and it seemed as if she could, in one great circle, see the whole world. She sat down on a large bare stone and thought about deep and mysterious things, wondering how the mountain was made, how long ago, what human feet had climbed to this very spot in ages past, and what the thoughts of these ancient men might have been. She wondered whether these first people, the Indians, had given the mountain a name to match its grandeur. Now she was the first white woman to stand on this spot and view this overwhelming sight, and the awesome thought made her feel small and humble.

It is in the northeastern corner of Sonoma County where it borders Lake and Napa Counties that this magnificent mountain rises to its height of 4,500 feet. Its slopes are thickly wooded. Its top is a series of volcanic pinnacles jagged, barren, and forbidding. But from its high slopes the climber of today can look to the south down the long Napa and Sonoma Valleys with their vineyards and fruit trees, stately old homes, and quiet living. Or look to the north and see the vast spread of quiet water that is Clear Lake. Or to the west and look out over a valley of steaming geysers, a fallen forest of petrified trees, and on to the tall living redwoods and pines that line the Russian River which flows down to the ocean. This mountain got its name in a most unusual way. According to legend, it was named three times by three different people who spoke three different languages and saw its beauty through the eyes of three entirely different cultures and ways of life.

The first known white man to look upon the mountain and give it a name was a man of God. In the history books there is only a sketchy record of his coming, vague references remembered by folk who seem to have forgotten even the holy father's name. He was a Spanish friar who had been sent into Northern California to seek out a new mission site. If the story is true, he was probably Father Jose Altamira, the man who founded the mission at Sonoma. Altamira was a young Franciscan fired with the zeal of his calling, which was to do for Northern California what Father Junipero Serra had done in establishing missions in other parts of California.

It was in the spring of 1823, and things had not been going so well for the mission in San Francisco. The ranches to the south that had provided its chief support were being taken away from the mission and set apart for settlers. Measles and tuberculosis had come with the white race and caused many deaths among the Indian converts. The mission of San Rafael Archangel had been established north of the bay, mainly because of its more healthful climate, to provide a pleasant place of rest for the weary and the sick from the other missions. But this was not enough. Father Altamira had been chosen to pick a place for a new mission to be established somewhere in the as yet unknown valleys to the north of San Rafael.

On the 25th of June he set out to explore the new country. On June 28 he entered the Valley of Sonoma and spent several days investigating it from side to side. He found conditions favorable — climate, location, an abundance of wood and stone, and most important of all, innumerable springs and streams. This valley, which the Indians called "Sonoma," was selected as the best site for the new mission; so on the morning of July 4, 1823, under a spreading oak at the base of the hills on the east side of the valley, he held the ceremony that marked the beginning of the mission.

Thus it was that Father Altamira settled in the valley where he could look up toward the beautiful mountain of our story. And as the now faint ancestral voices echo it, after a few moments of fixed observation there flashed to his mind a recollection of a tomb in an old abbey he had known back in Europe, the Abbey of Rheims. For what he saw in the form of the mountain, etched in silhouette from the rugged formations near the top, was the figure of a sleeping woman, one of the Saints lying on her bier just as it looked in the artistic carvings in the old chapel that he remembered. In his imagination he saw there what many later visitors have seen, the effigy of the reclining Saint, true in detail even to the graceful flowing lines that resemble the form of a woman lying in death. With this picture for his inspiration it is said that he gave the mountain its name, the name of the sleeping Saint.

The second person to come to the mountain and give it a name was a Russian princess. Eighteen years had passed since the mission was established at Sonoma, and now it was 1841. Russian hunters and trappers had been operating out of Fort Ross since 1812, or possibly even earlier, but by now international complications had reached such a point and pressure had built up against the Russians

80

to such an extent that they were thinking of withdrawing from the California coast. Having taken the best of the furs by that time, there was very little to keep them there, anyway. The Russian governor — or, more accurately, the resident manager — was Baron Alexander Rotchef, a poet, traveler, stubborn business man, and the husband of a beautiful vivacious princess whose godfather was none other than Czar Nicholas himself. It was the princess who had wanted to come to California in the first place and had asked the Czar to appoint her husband as governor of this wild frontier outpost. She was not afraid of the Indians; she looked forward to the rigors of the primitive frontier life she would live here — primitive, that is, in comparison to the luxuries of the court of the Russian Emperor.

She loved to take long rides into the countryside, but in this wild land there was danger in such freedom. It was rumored that Mexican troops were on their way from San Francisco to expel the Russians and take over Fort Ross. Don Mariano Vallejo had been sent as commissionado to the Pueblo Sonoma with a force of soldiers to serve as a warning to the Russians as well as to bring the Indians under subjugation in that region. He was only a lieutenant at first, but rapidly advanced to Commandant General and has been known as "General" ever since. He conquered the Indian Chief Solano, and in the spring of 1841 paid a diplomatic visit to Fort Ross.

The Russian governor and his princess received the Mexican commander with all the politeness and hospitality that any royal court could have extended, and Vallejo responded with equal courtesy. The vanquished Indian chief Solano even came forward when the Mexican leader gave him permission to do so, to extend his greeting and offer a gift to the princess — a long mantle made of blue feathers. She gazed in rapture at this truly magnificent gift. The Indian never took his eyes off the princess. The Russian governor spoke of furs, and the Mexican general listened. The Russian spoke of the Indians, and the Mexican officer told of his success in conquering them. The Mexican invited the Russians to pay him a return visit for a fiesta at Sonoma, and the Russian governor accepted. And through it all, the silent Solano stared at the beautiful woman.

Later that year the governor and his lady, escorted by a small party of Russians, made their courtesy call upon General Vallejo at Sonoma. They were received with calculated politeness, and the fiesta was a great success. The conquered Chief Solano, now turned

Christian under Vallejo's supervision, was always somewhere close to the Russian guests. And always he looked at the princess. Toward the end of the visit he came forward with a gift which clearly indicated that he wanted her to become his wife. He was rejected, and although the embarrassment of the moment was handled with diplomacy and tact, the proud Indian burned under the humiliation.

The visit was pleasant and socially successful, but its more serious purpose was to make it clear that the Russians must withdraw from Fort Ross. Governor Rotchef was of the same mind, and upon receiving approval from home, he sold the fort to John Sutter and preparations were begun for the governor and his princess to go back to Russia. But on their excursion to Sonoma, this woman who loved the wild beauty of California had seen the mountain and felt its invitation and its challenge. Its summit was like a magnet from which she could not turn away. She could not leave without climbing the mountain.

By coincidence at that particular time, of some visiting Russian scientists who had come to Sonoma from San Francisco brought her the opportunity she needed. They were there to climb the mountain on a collecting trip, and she arranged to go along. The little expedition splashed across the lowland streams, made their way up the wooded slopes, and slowly climbed to the steep upper part of the mountain where its six mighty domes of pumice, lava, and obsidian stood bare. Finally they reached the summit, the first white people to scale the top. They looked off to the west and saw the endless blue of the Pacific Ocean. Far off to the east was the snowcapped Sierra Nevada. The lady stood at last on top of the world and thought of the power of God, the grandeur of nature, and the generations of Indians who must also have climbed to that spot. They raised the Russian flag and built a high cairn of lava rock. On the pile they placed a copper plate inscribed with their names, the date, and the name of the Russian princess, which was to be the name of the mountain.

On their way back from this expedition the Russian party was captured by the Indians. Chief Solano, still infatuated by the lady's beauty, was determined to make the white lady his wife. Solano had kidnapped wives before and would gladly have killed all the men in the party in order to remove any obstacle that stood between him and the woman he wanted. Fortunately for the princess, General Vallejo arrived just in time to rescue her from the Indian. She returned to Fort Ross, and early the next year when the Fort was sold she went back to Russia.

The third person to look up toward the mountain and give it a name was far from being either a priest or a lady. He was a plain, rough-mannered, far sighted American sea captain named Stephen Smith. In 1844 he secured from the Mexican Governor Micheltorena a grant of over 35,000 acres, land that had been occupied by the Russians on the coast, known as the Rancho Bodega. In the redwood region east of Bodega he set up a sawmill. He looked up at the mighty redwoods and saw wealth. He looked out toward the harbor where his sailing ship lay at anchor and saw in the ship a symbol of the robust life and romantic memories of his adventures at sea. And he looked far inland toward the mountain and saw the majestic beauty that had inspired others before him. And it is said that it was the name of his ship which he gave also to the mountain.

So it happened that the central character of our story was named at least three times. And the folk will tell you that fate must have had a hand in the christening because each of the three had given the mountain the same name — Saint Helena. The first one, the priest, saw in it the sculptured image of Saint Helena as he remembered it from sacred carvings in Europe. The second one, the princess, gave the mountain her own name, which was Helena Gagarin Rotchef. And the third one, the sea captain called Smith, took the name of his ship on whose bow was painted *St. Helena.*

It has been told many times, and is written somewhere, that each of these persons happened upon the name without knowing that anyone else had had the same thought. It makes a good story, but the more scrupulous historians do not believe it to be entirely true. The records of Father Altamira and other explorers of the region were known at the Mission of Solano in the pueblo of Sonoma when Helena Gagarin Rotchef and her husband visited General Vallejo there. She must have known the name before she climbed the mountain, and the coincidence must have led her on. And Captain Smith's ship, the *St. Helena,* he had obtained from the Russians who had abandoned Bodega Bay and who might very well have named the ship after the mountain or the lady or the saint.

But whether the story is true or not, it is a tale that adds something to the grandeur and beauty of this remarkable mountain. and so today, the next time you drive over that winding highway up the slopes of Mt. St. Helena from Calistoga to Middletown, think of the mountain, the name, and the story. Perhaps, after all, fate did lend a hand at the christening.

Fifteen Seconds to Kill

Do you remember the old ballad about the feuding Martins and the Coys?

> Oh, the Martins and the Coys,
> They were reckless mountain boys ...

They were really the Hatfields and the McCoys, but that doesn't matter. They just about eliminated each other before a boy and a girl finally stopped the killing.

> He was set to pull the trigger
> When he saw her pretty figger.
> And he knew that love had kicked him in the face.

This supposedly ended the feud and united the two families in battles that were a little less mortal.

Then there was the historic fight at the O.K. Corral in Tombstone, when the Earp brothers and Doc Holliday took care of the bad guys of the Clanton outfit. They shot up Ike and Billy Clanton and the McLowery brothers to a fare-thee-well. In that battle, which lasted less than thirty seconds, a total of thirty-four shots were exchanged, three men were killed and three were wounded. You hear about that fight all over the West. But that was just a Sunday School picnic compared to a shoot-out that occurred on the streets of Willits — it was called Little Lake then — a little over a hundred years ago when the Frosts took on the Coateses. The carnage was terrific — six dead and three wounded, and all in about fifteen seconds of gunplay. Now, that was real feuding.

The 11th of October, 1867, was as good a day as any for a fight. It looked as though Wesley Coates was drinking himself into the right mood, and the people of Little Lake knew just about what to expect. Wesley was twenty-five years old, lean, hard, and mean clear through. When he was drunk he could fight a buzz saw and turn it himself. This was going to be his day, and he had his twin brother, Henry, to back him up. The Coateses were a wild and desperate tribe around Mendocino County in those days. And on this particular day they were all in town. There was old Thomas, about sixty-three, and his brother Abner, a little younger, both as tough a breed as ever came out of Wisconsin. Then there was Abner's son Albert and his cousin Abraham, both about twenty-one. And finally there were the three brothers — Wesley, Henry, and James. They were all Coateses, all armed and all dangerous.

That's the way it was when a man named Duncan came to town. Duncan was a peace-loving man, never in any kind of trouble — except that he had a large family. He had married one of the Frost girls, and that was in itself an entangling alliance because the Frosts were a fighting family, too, just as bad as the Coateses. And these two sides hated each other like a Campbellite preacher hates the Devil. To make matters worse, Wesley Coates had cast eyes on one of the Duncan girls, and what he saw gave him certain ideas. He made his brag around town that some dark night he was going to steal that filly out of old man Duncan's corral just for the fun of it. In fact, it was rumored that he had already done it.

Anyway, when Duncan came to town on this October day in 1867, Wesley got him into a fight. Some say it was an argument about the Civil War that started it; some say otherwise. Anyway, with six other members of his family to back him up, Wesley felt like roughing Duncan up a little, and it didn't take him long to do it. Most of the fight took place out in the street in front of Kirk Brier's store and saloon, and for a while it was fairly even. But Wesley knocked Duncan out, and the other Coateses stood there watching while Wesley walked over and picked up Duncan's gun, which had fallen out of its holster. He broke the gun open and dumped the bullets on the ground.

That's the way it was when three of the Frosts rode up. They were not expected, or Wesley would never have goaded Duncan into a fight, for the Frosts were tough customers to go up against. Three of them might just equal seven Coateses if the wind was right. Elisha Frost was forty-three and about as tough as a Missouri mule. With him were his two nephews, Martin, about of an age with the younger Coates boys, and the kid Isom, who was only sixteen but as good a shot as you could ever want to find. They were all three armed with Colt's revolvers.

So when they rode up, this is what they saw: Elisha Frost's brother-in-law, Duncan, lying in the street as if dead, with Wesley Coates standing over him holding a gun. The six other Coateses stood watching, and the crowd of spectators formed a half circle further back. The situation spoke for itself. Abner Coates had a double-barreled shotgun, one barrel rifled and one smooth for shot. When the Frosts rode up and jumped from their horses, old Abner

86

Coates knew that trouble had arrived. Perhaps he only wanted to keep the Frosts from interfering with a fistfight; perhaps not. No one knows. But whatever his motives, he raised his shotgun and leveled it at Elisha Frost. Before he could pull the triggers, Elisha drew; so Abner shot him with the shotgun, giving him both barrels.

The instant the first shot was fired, Martin Frost opened up on the Coateses. Almost before they knew what was happening, Martin had dropped three of them: Wesley, Abraham, and Henry. The boy Isom, the youngest Frost, opened fire on Thomas, the oldest of the Coateses, and Thomas went down. When Elisha Frost fell from the shotgun blast, he missed his shot at Abner, but as he lay dying he managed to put one into young Albert Coates. Duncan still lay on the ground, and it was discovered later that Wesley had stabbed him in their fight before the shooting started.

The gunfight from beginning to end took exactly fifteen seconds, and the only words spoken were from Abner Coates when he cried out, "My God!" That was when Elisha Frost had killed his young son Albert. The aim of the Frosts had been good. According to Dr. Thomas L. Barnes, who examined the bodies later, Henry Coates had been killed by a single bullet that entered his chest, ranging toward the spine. Wesley took three shots: one through the body near the heart, one through the left arm, and one on the head but not penetrating the skull. Abraham Coates was wounded with two shots in the chest and died six days later. These were the six shots fired by Martin Frost.

Young Isom Frost made his shots count, too. Two of them entered the body, one very near the heart of Thomas Coates. Either one would have proved fatal. And Elisha Frost, who lay dying, managed to put two bullets into Albert Coates. One of them went directly through the heart.

For some reason the Coateses had concentrated their fire on Elisha. The examining doctor counted thirty-eight pieces of shot in his body, extending from the nipples to the upper part of the thighs. These were from the first shotgun blast of Abner's that brought him down. After this he took five more slugs in the body before a sixth bullet, straight through the heart, finished him. Martin and Isom Frost were not hit. Abner and James Coates were wounded, but not killed. Mr. Duncan recovered from his knife wound.

So the score for that terrible quarter of a minute stood: the Coateses, five dead or fatally wounded, and two bleeding pretty badly; the Frosts, one dead and two not even scratched. When it was over, these mortal enemies, one Frost and five Coateses, lay side by side on the street of their little town. And today they are all sleeping, almost side by side, in the little graveyard known as Sawyer's Cemetery near Willits.

The feud between these families had been of long standing. What caused it in the beginning, no one knows. The fight with Duncan was only the minor episode that brought it to a climax. Both families were known to be mean fighters, and it was rumored that the Frosts had been doing some killing back in Missouri before they came west. Martin Frost had a brother, Elijah, who was not present for the shooting of the Coateses; but he was present in 1879 when some "Mendocino outlaws" were lynched at a bridge near Ten Mile not far from Willits. He was one of those who got hanged.

Then in 1884 James Frost, the son of Elisha, who took so many bullets from the Coateses in 1867, got in a quarrel over land, and James deliberately shot his enemy through the head. And who was his victim? None other than his own uncle, the man we've been talking about, Martin Frost.

Young Isom Frost lived on to an old age. Long after the affair with the Coateses, he told a neighbor, "I didn't know what was happening, it all happened so fast. When I saw Abner Coates draw his shotgun up and fire and I heard Martin shooting too, I just drew and fired. It seemed a matter of life and death, and I didn't know what was going on. I didn't want to kill nobody." Isom was also present that day in 1884 when James gunned down his brother Martin. So Isom began to trail his nephew James. At last one day he caught him and killed him. This time the law took a hand, and Isom was sent to prison for a long time. But when he returned, and the years wore on, he was remembered as a sweet and kindly and gentle old man whose violent past was almost too unreal to believe. He always carried a rifle, though, even to the end.

But let's go back to the two families, the Coateses and the Frosts, on that fatal day in 1867. The folk will say that it was the women of both houses who came forth and claimed the bodies of their men. Only two of the dead men were married, but they all had sisters. It is said, too — and this may be gospel truth — that the feud of these two families was ended, not by the killings on that October day, but by romance. One of the girls from the Coates side actually

88

fell in love with a boy whose name was Frost. They were married, and their descendants still live somewhere in California.

William B. Ide, the Hero of Sonoma

It was a beautiful morning in May, 1846. The upper Sacramento Valley lay rich and fertile in the hot summer sun, and the ranchers and farmers were pleased with the prospect of bounteous crops and fat cattle that year. One such rancher, William B. Ide, was well known in this part of the valley, and on this particular morning he was out working in his field. He did not see the lone rider that entered his gate and, without dismounting, held a brief conversation with Mrs. Ide in the dooryard.

"Daniel," said Mrs. Ide to the oldest son, who lounged nearby listening, "go down and tell your pa he's wanted. And tell him to hurry up; he ain't got all day." The boy scampered off, and soon Ide appeared riding one of the horses still in harness.

After a hasty conversation with the stranger, Ide said, "Daniel, go saddle up my good horse and then unharness these nags and put them in the shed. Ma, go in and get my gun. I've got to go. Dan will know what to do about the crops if I don't get back. No telling when that will be." Mrs. Ide understood and obeyed. These were serious times despite the rich promise of the valley, for trouble was brewing between the American settlers and the Mexicans who, after all, were the legal masters of the country. So when her husband and his companion rode out of the yard on this quiet morning, it would be seven months before she would see him again.

Ide was an unusual man. Not much was known about him except that he was a New Englander. He had decided to come west, like so many others, to find a new home. He brought cattle along, a small herd of breeding stock to get started in ranching. He brought three well-equipped wagons, his five children, and his old dog. And his wife. They joined a wagon train and wheeled westward across the prairies and mountains, heading for Oregon.

When they reached Fort Hall, Idaho, Ide changed his plans and turned toward California. He came down the Humboldt, across the Sierra Nevada Mountains to Sutter's Fort, and from there he worked his way up the Sacramento River to a stopping place just below the Red Bluffs. From a man named Josiah Belden he secured 30,000 acres of good range land and rich valley loam along the river. Later, after gold was discovered, he and his boys went up into the mountains and made a strike good enough to enable them to pan out $25,000 in gold, which he used to pay off the ranch. Thus he became the clear owner of one of the larger ranches in the valley, located just south of Red Bluff.

But it was a little earlier than this — in 1846 — that something more important happened. Fear and frustration agitated the Californians. Lieutenant John C. Fremont was here with a small company of soldiers on a mysterious mission. He had something in the back of his mind about winning California for the United States. The Mexican military leader, General Castro, had let it be known that the American settlers were not welcome, and the word went out that he was beginning a campaign to expel them by force if necessary. There were many rumors that General Castro was preparing to raid the American settlers, confiscate their property, and drive them out. All this was in the minds of Ide and his companion as they rode away from the rancher's dooryard.

The men rode southward down the valley, meeting up with several of their friends along the way. All the settlers shared the same alarm. The time had come for them to defend their homes against General Castro. As the little company grew, joined by more men from ranches down the river, the opinion was beginning to form that an offensive action might prove more successful than defense. But their immediate objective was to meet and confer with Lieutenant Fremont, who was waiting for them at the Buttes near Marysville. More men had come in from other parts of the valley, and a camp was made. For the moment Fremont was undecided what to do. The United States was not yet at war with Mexico, and Fremont was not telling anybody what his real mission was in California. But he knew what was about to happen, that California was destined to come into the United States one way or another, preferably in peace, but by war if necessary.

For the time being, Fremont could not act, but there was no reason why these bold men from up the valley could not be used for his secret purpose, so he incited them to make a raid on Sonoma, the capitol of the northern section of Mexican California — a raid that was to prove historic indeed. Some of these men were adventurers who had everything to gain and nothing to lose — just a gang of overgrown juvenile delinquents out for plunder or excitement. But some of them, like Ide, were idealists who had the thought that a nation could be built here, and they had the dream that they might help make the beginning.

So, leaving Fremont at the Buttes, they headed southward stealthily and by night to Sonoma. Just at dawn on the fourteenth of June, 1846, they silently crept up to the plaza in that little Mexican town. That was the strategic place to command the town and was not far from where General Vallejo, the Commander of the Mexican northern outpost, lived. After a brief conference it was decided that they should send in some of their party to demand the General's surrender. So two or three of the adventurers went into Vallejo's home, and the door closed behind them. Inside, they found that the General was not up yet. He came down to meet them in his nightshirt, and as soon as he saw them he realized what was happening. He excused himself, went back to his room, put on his finest uniform, and came down again. He presented himself to them formally, and in solemn grandeur he drew his sabre and offered it to them in surrender.

But the untrained rednecks didn't know what to do with that sabre. They looked at each other, uncertain of what was expected of them. They had no leader to receive the official surrender, so they did not accept the sword. The General politely set to one side the symbol of his surrender and in true Mexican hospitality he opened his liquor cabinet. He brought out wines and brandies for refreshment, and the weary conquerors sat down to drink the matter over and perhaps outline plans for the next step — that is, if there was to be a next step.

Time went by. Out in the street the victorious invaders continued to wait. The doors remained closed, and no one could guess what was happening inside. Finally they sent in another man. They said, "Captain Grisby, go in and see what's going on." So he went in, and they sat down to wait some more. But Grisby did not return. They waited. Nothing happened. Finally in desperation they said, "Ide, you go in there and find out what's going on. And for heaven's sake come back out and tell us."

William B. Ide went into the house, and there he discovered what had happened. The liquor had been served, and most of it had been consumed. One of the patriots was a little too dizzy to talk or listen. Another was practically asleep, and a third was solemnly going over some hastily devised articles of surrender. General Vallejo was calmly waiting for the whole proceeding to come to an end.

With the surrender of General Vallejo, the Americans had a republic on their hands. But then they didn't know what to do with it. "What's the word from Fremont?" they asked, looking around at each other. But nobody had received any word from Fremont. What was to be done next? Some were for abandoning the campaign then and there and getting away. But it was too late for that. They said, "If we give the General back to the Mexicans now, we'll be in for it for sure. They'll cut our throats, that's what."

Obviously, a leader was needed. This was the moment that destiny had chosen for Ide. Here within his grasp was fame and perhaps, fortune. It was as Shakespeare once said, "Some are born great, some achieve greatness, and some have greatness thrust upon them." William B. Ide was a man who was not born to greatness. Every once in a while in his career in California he worked hard to achieve success, and occasionally he had the eminence of leadership thrust upon him — or almost. But every time he had power just within his reach, he failed to grasp it or hold it very long. He had a strange mixture of characteristics — the combined high seriousness and nobility of purpose of the idealist, and with it was the comic spirit of the frontier. He also had more than his share of Christian humility, a virtue that always interfered with his rise to greatness.

At this moment, with leadership thrust upon him, Ide rose. The situation was grim. "Boys," he said, "we've gone too far; there's no turning back now. The die has been cast. We must go through with what we started." And so Ide and a few others made plans to form a Republic of California. Naturally, a flag was needed, so a flag was created — an emblem suddenly inspired and of course home made. The flag was made out of muslin, probably an old flour sack. They put a star in one corner — perhaps out of respect for the boys from Texas in the party. They made a red flannel bar to spread across the bottom, and the words "Republic of California" were painted in. In the center was a big grizzly bear — not rampant, but planted solidly on all fours. The natives standing around watching this creation thought it was supposed to be a picture of a pig, but these opinions were prudently kept private. The flag, however, served its purpose. It was the sacred symbol of the conquering heroes, who as yet didn't know what to do with what they had conquered. That original Bear Flag unfortunately was lost in the San Francisco fire of 1906.

William B. Ide was now the leader, and with due regard for his office he was immediately seized with a fit of writing. From him

94

came numerous proclamations stating the purpose of his new government. One of these was " ... to establish and perpetuate a liberal, a just, and honorable government which shall secure to all civil, religious, and personal liberty, which shall insure the security of life and property, which shall detect and punish crime and injustice, which shall encourage industry, virtue, and literature, and which shall foster agriculture, manufactures, and mechanism by guaranteeing freedom to commerce." So proclaimed the first President of California.

He was not only President of the Republic, he was also Commander-in-Chief of the defending forces — an army of some twenty or twenty-five men. But the army had nothing to do except protect and hold what they had — the town of Sonoma, over which the Bear Flag waved. It was General Castro whom the conquerors now feared. Not knowing that, far from being an immediate threat to them, Castro was down at San Francisco Bay preparing to get out of that part of the country, Ide and his men made ready to defend against attack. One night they heard horses approaching, so they brought out their captured cannons and aimed them off into the darkness toward the approaching party. They lit their torches and stood ready to fire at the invaders. But suddenly a voice came out of the darkness: "Don't shoot, boys! It's us." It was Kit Carson, leading Fremont and his men into the camp at Sonoma. He had yelled just in time to prevent a fiasco that might have been fatal to Fremont.

After notice was received of the formal surrender of Mexico to the United States, Fremont took over the command at Sonoma and raised the American flag. Then it was his job to go south and consolidate the country and engage Castro if necessary. He recruited a company of volunteers to make the trip, and William B. Ide joined. The Commander-in-Chief of the forces of the Republic became a private in Fremont's company. Moreover, he had to give up his beautiful horse to Fremont, and he walked all the way to Los Angeles. In August when the American flag was raised in Los Angeles, Ide was there, and soon afterward when he was mustered out of the army, he started working his way north again toward home. But he didn't have either horse or money, and by the time he reached the Sacramento River near Sutter's Fort he was tired, ragged, hungry, and eager to get home.

He found a riverboat ready to start up the river, and having no money, he offered to work for his passage.

"Can you saw wood?" the captain asked.

"I've cut a great deal of wood in my day," said Ide, "and I can cut wood now." So he began to saw wood for his passage home. Someone recognized Ide and told the captain who he was.

"Mr. Ide," the captain apologized, "you can go home free of charge if you want to. You don't have to work."

"No," said Ide, "a bargain's a bargain. I'll saw wood." And saw wood he did until he got up the river to Red Bluff and home.

For the next few years he held many offices in his county — sometimes several of them at the same time. The county seat was the old town of Monroeville south of Red Bluff, and apparently Ide spent much of his time there on county business. He was remembered as a very practical man, a trait which folklore can document in the story of Ide and his jail.

Monroeville needed a jail. Prisoners were escaping, and something had to be done about it. So the county appropriated $600 to buy a new jail. Ide had hoped to get a good iron cell from San Francisco and have it shipped up the river, but he found that the $600 would not cover the cost. He had been a carpenter, and he had his tools, so he said, "All right, I'll make the jail myself." He got the lumber, some iron bars and nuts and bolts, he sawed and hammered and bolted, and he made the jail. He planted it in plain sight out under a big oak at the edge of town. It was a very well-ventilated jail, and the prisoners could sit in it and look out at the village, and the citizens could watch the prisoners. It was a huge success.

Ide was also said to have been a man who didn't know the meaning of fear. Folk tell the story of how some horse thieves came along one night and got away with several of Ide's best horses. A posse was formed and the search began. Ide and his son were riding with the posse part of the way, but then they separated and the Ides went a different way. They were riding along a ridge when, looking down in a little valley, they saw the camp of the horse thieves with the horses in plain sight. Ide started toward them.

"Pa, we'd better wait for the posse. If we get up too close these fellows will shoot us."

"No," said Ide. "Those are our horses, and we've come to get them. So let's go down and get them." They rode in on the outlaws, who pulled their guns and drew down on the two.

"Don't come any closer," they yelled, "or we'll shoot you."

"I don't think you will," answered Ide. "After all, these are our horses and we're here to get them." He dismounted and walked toward them. "You know," he said calmly, "back behind me a little way there's a posse coming. Now, I don't believe in lynching, but I'll bet that if you're around when they get here there'll be a hanging." He walked over and untied his horses. When he turned around, the horse thieves were just going over the hill as hard as they could ride.

On a new frontier things happen fast, time seems to get compressed and a lifetime can be lived in a few short years. Ide went to Sonoma as a patriot of the new land within a year after he arrived in California, and he reached the end of his career and met his death less than seven years after he moved west. Time seemed to tighten itself around him.

In the winter of 1852 Ide was lying in a little cabin near Monroeville, apparently all alone and sick with smallpox. He had under his pillow the key to the county safe containing the county money and some of his own. Someone managed to get the key away from him and rob the safe. A posse pursued immediately and recovered the county's money, but apparently nobody thought to recover Ide's money. Some folk will tell you that he had his money himself and that he didn't die of smallpox in that lonely cabin but was murdered and robbed, and that someone buried him in a lonely grave near the river and put the mark of smallpox on it so no one would disturb it. But no one knows for sure where he was buried. Ide had been called the "Hero of Sonoma," and yet his contemporaries never took him seriously. He is a patron saint to many people in Northern California, and yet no one can describe him. There isn't known to be a picture of him in existence.

Today, a small adobe house sits on a high river bank, with a deep cool well beside the door and a broad oak spreading its shade over house and yard. The wide valley lying warm and rich under the California sun spreads off to the south, sloping gently down to the Sacramento River. This is a real place. At this spot today, as it was a hundred years ago, the river is deep and slow, heavy and powerful, its blue water lined with the green of vines and trees on either side. To the east the hills rise abruptly and become mountains; to the south is the prosperous, growing city of Red Bluff. And the little house itself is known as the William B. Ide Adobe.

When Malay Pete Went Up

The discovery of gold in California was an explosion heard around the world. And the fallout from the blast sprinkled down on the big cities and the country towns of America, Europe, South America, and Asia — the whole world. Most of the people that the fabulous reports fell on became a little touched, and those who felt it most caught a great fever and began a stampede to California to acquire some of this gold for themselves.

One little bit of this magic matter floated and drifted and finally came to rest on the black head of a poor native of one of the farthest little islands in the farthest part of the Pacific Ocean. He, too, caught the fever, and turned his wondering eyes toward California; and although he had earned an honest living that kept him honorably undernourished as a sail maker in his little fishing village in Malaya, he turned his back on the dignity of his poverty and set his sails for America.

Of course, the sails he set were not actually his own. He merely worked his passage to California by mending sails on a large freighter that stopped at his island once or twice a year. His one-man migration was not exactly what could be called a stampede, and yet within his heart there burned the same fire, and in his mind he dreamed the same dreams, as thousands of others who came with the gold rush.

And thus it was that Malay Pete got to San Francisco in 1850. He jumped ship there, which was an acceptable thing to do, he thought, because everyone else was jumping ship. He worked his way up to Oroville, which was the intelligent thing to do because everybody knew that gold was to be found there. And, beside a little stream far up in a canyon east of Oroville, he built a little cabin. So the little man lived in his little cabin beside the little stream and panned a little gold. Pete came to town once in awhile to buy supplies, but for the most part he preferred to stay to himself. The people left him that way, and the years passed — forty years or more.

Then came that great and wonderful day in the summer of 1893. Pete had come to town for supplies as usual, but to his amazement, something strange was happening. A big crowd had gathered at the edge of town to watch an odd looking man doing a crazy thing. He was a self-proclaimed "traveling scientist," and Pete sensed that the crazy fellow was the object of respect among the people watching him. The scientist had a kind of furnace going, and from it a long tube led to a large sphere that was growing larger and larger as it filled with the hot air. Before long the huge ball was pulling at its anchor ropes, and a little basket dangled beneath it almost touching the ground.

Apparently heedless of personal danger, the brave scientist climbed into the basket and gave a signal to the attendants who had charge of the anchor ropes. All at once, the great ball with the dangling basket carrying the fearless man rose up into the air and continued to rise higher and higher. Malay Pete stared in wonder and awe. The crowd voiced its approval, and the balloon ascended higher and grew smaller, drifting off toward the southwest. Pete could hardly see it now, a moving speck in the sky.

The people waited. Pete waited. He heard voices around him saying, "I'll bet a feller could go a hundred miles in one o' them things."

"Yes, if the wind was right you might even float clear to China. Who knows?"

At that moment an idea began to germinate in Pete's head. And when the balloon gradually descended to the ground again and it was established that the flying scientist was indeed safe and sound, the idea in Pete's mind had sprouted, taken root, and was beginning to grow.

Pete went back to his little cabin in the hills and dug up his sack of gold dust. He hurried to town again and went to the store. He bought a lot of canvas, some thread and needles, and rushed back to his cabin. Pete's days were still spent panning gold because he needed a little capital to work on, but at nights he gathered his materials around him and began to sew, making sure that the canvas pieces fitted together very tightly, so tightly that no air could escape. Malay Pete was making a balloon.

As Pete worked, his thoughts floated skyward. He dreamed of flying home to his little fishing village in Malaya as a great and rich and wise man, arriving from the skies like a god. His old friends would flock around him, and he would be kind to them. He would show them his gold, and with his great wealth he would be generous. The whole village would admire and perhaps even worship him, and when he died he would have a great funeral and his body would at last return to the soil of his birth.

It came to pass that after several months of hard work, the balloon was finished. The stars had shifted in the heavens, the seasons had turned, and it was now December; in fact, it was

100

Christmas Day when the whole thing was ready. This was a good omen, Pete thought. He packed himself a lunch and put his cabin in order. After all, he might want to return some day and get a little more gold from the river. He carefully closed the door and went out to where his great scientific achievement was anchored. It had been attached to a proper furnace to which was attached a long pipe that led to the bottom of the big canvas bag. He built a good fire and waited. Slowly the bag filled with hot air and smoke. To the bottom of the bag he had tied a chair, the more comfortable of his two cabin chairs, and the whole contraption was pretty well anchored to an old stump nearby.

As the sphere slowly inflated, Pete could see that this experiment was going to be a success. He was a scientist now, no less successful than the one from whom he had taken his only lesson. He climbed into the chair and waited. No crowd stood by to cheer him, but such is sometimes the lonely fate of the scholar. At last the time came when the balloon was tugging at the rope, pulling like a ship trying to drift with the tide. When Pete judged that the right moment had arrived, he reached down and cut the rope below. Up he went! Up to the treetops and far above! Up almost to the clouds! In his mind he was headed for home, and he was happy.

A brisk wind was blowing, all right, but not to the southwest toward the great ocean and Malaya. In fact, it was in the very opposite direction, to the northeast, that the air currents were carrying the balloon and Pete in his chair dangling under it. They were completely off course, heading for the Sierra Nevada Mountains. The gravity of this navigational error was soon apparent, and the horror of its consequences was beginning to freeze into his mind when another thing happened. In an instant Pete learned what many a scientist has learned from bitter experience — that a space traveler must depend upon the perfect functioning of even the slightest part of his machine and there can be no human error. Malay Pete — scientist, mining magnate, rich man, air-borne traveler, and the would-be idol of all the people in his village — learned too late. The dreadful thing happened.

Two men from Oroville who chanced to be riding in the hills that day watched the disaster unfold, but they couldn't believe what they were seeing. Sailing through the skies above them was a strange apparition and part of it was human.

"Well, I do believe it's a balloon — or some such like contraption," said Charles Topping as he stopped his horse to watch in wonder. And his companion, known as Lem Dunlap, took off his hat, scratched his head and grinned.

"I'll be ding-busted if that ain't a crazy galoot up there a-ridin' under that thing," he pronounced with amusement. And that was the exact moment when disaster struck. The entire balloon suddenly burst into flame and fell in a stream of smoke among the trees behind a distant ridge. A spark from Pete's furnace had been sucked into the bag, and eventually the canvas had ignited. The two watchers saw the sudden flames and the great puff of smoke it made when the balloon collapsed and went down — somewhere in the rugged Sierra foothills.

Topping was speechless, but Dunlap had recourse to a few carefully selected words: "Well, I'll be a cock-eyed, hammered-down, sawed-off, knock-kneed, pigeon-toed son of a sea cook!"

The witnesses immediately reported the occurrence in town, and a search party was organized to find the unfortunate victim. No trace of the wrecked aircraft could be found. In fact, the two men almost began to doubt their own story because, you see, it was Christmas, Day and it hadn't been an entirely dry Christmas. They had cause to wonder whether they had really seen anything or not.

But the next day the search was continued, and it chanced that some of the searching party happened to pass Malay Pete's little cabin. It didn't take much figuring to piece out what had happened after they found what was left of the scientific experiment — the furnace, the piece of rope, the canvas trimmings, and the abandoned cabin. The people knew, then, that Malay Pete had "gone up." The rescue party gave up the search and headed back to town, concluding that little old Pete was dead. The local newspaper ran his obituary, as was proper in such cases, and that, they thought, was the end of Pete.

But it wasn't. A few days later a couple of prospectors came into town bearing a sorry burden which they delivered to the County Hospital. It was Pete. It seems that when his balloon had fallen, Pete had got himself dumped into the trees. The shreds of the canvas and the ropes had caught in a pine tree, the chair was dangling from the branches, and poor Pete had been dumped out in the river. Stunned, bruised, half drowned, and half frozen, he had lain in the river for several hours and would certainly have perished if the prospectors had not come along.

Pete's sojourn in the hospital was brief. He was just too tough to die, said his friends. But the spirit, somehow, had gone out of him. He went back to his cabin yard and tore down the scientific laboratory, his furnace. Then he got out his old gold pan and went to work in the river again. People used to stop and talk to him after that whenever they were passing his way. He was always cordial enough, but there was one subject that he would never talk about his ill-fated balloon flight. Along with the balloon, his great dream had collapsed, and he knew that he would never see his little Malayan fishing village again. After more than forty years of loneliness, Pete's yearning, homesick heart had led him to a magnificent adventure. His failure had been magnificent, too.

Eventually, in his time, Malay Pete sank into an unknown grave. He went home as only the humble dead can go. But there is at least one distinction that his story must record: Malay Pete was the first aeronautic casualty in the Sierra Nevada Mountains.

Sontag and Evans

It was early fall, and the annual deer hunt was on. I had hunted with Ace Morgan for five years, and we always got our deer. Although we went into the mountains prepared to stay the entire season, we never actually camped out more than four or five days because we always "filled up," as the saying was, early and without too much effort. Ace was that kind of hunter. He knew the habits of the deer and where they could be found. Consequently, we had ample time to spend in camp, and in the evenings after a bracing drink or two and a belly-tight dinner, we were usually in the mood to sit around and listen to some of Ace's stories.

That's how I happened to get the saga of Sontag and Evans. Ace Morgan had made himself an authority on the subject of these two California outlaws, and I was glad when the conversation — encouraged by the campfire, the rugged mountains, and the basic comfort inside us — worked itself around to the story.

"Yeah. I didn't know Sontag and Evans personally, you understand," he explained as he lit a pipe. "That was back before my time. I got it from my grandad, and he got it right from the horse's mouth. I guess you'd say he *was* the horse's mouth on that one; he knew 'em, and they were the wildest outlaws that ever come out of the San Joaquin Valley. Even when I was a boy, the kids didn't play cowboys and Indians; they played Sontag and Evans." Ace stirred the fire and settled back to tell a story that he had repeated many times and knew by heart.

"It seems that Chris Evans had come to California back in the 1870s, and he bought some land owned by the railroad over near Visalia. Like a lot of farmers at that time, he thought he was buying the land for two-and-a-half an acre — that's what the railroad told him — but when he went to pay for it after a few years of putting improvements on it, he found that the railroad wanted to charge more than he could pay — maybe ten or fifteen dollars an acre by then, with the improvements and all. Chris Evans and the other farmers got together and raised cain about it, but it didn't do 'em no good. The railroad owned the valley and the banks and the politicians, so they got nowhere. Naturally, they turned sour on the railroad — got real bitter about it. But it seemed like there was nothing they could do but pay up or lose their land.

"Then one day Chris Evans met another man that hated the railroad about as much as he did. That was John Sontag. He had worked for the railroad and had had some kind of accident that put him out of commission, and instead of helping and taking care of him, the railroad had fired him — kicked him right off the premises. So Sontag and Evans got to be pretty good friends.

"Not long after that, as Chris Evans, John Sontang and his brother George were walking along the streets of Visalia, a crippled engine with a wrecked express car limped into Fresno. The train had been wrecked by some robbers near Collis. Rumors had it that at least $50,000 had been stolen. Some of the loot was in Peruvian silver coin that could easily be identified. This was about the fourth robbery the railroad company had had in that part of the country, and they were getting pretty sore about it. Well, they knew how Sontag and Evans felt about 'em, so the railroad detectives got suspicious and started asking questions. They found out that Sontag and Evans had not been in Visalia the night of the robbery at Collis. One of 'em had hired a team from the livery stable and it was said they went into the mountains the evening before the robbery. Then both of 'em showed up in Visalia the night after. One of their horses had lost a shoe, which was a dead give-away, and a posse followed the trail of the robbers till it led 'em almost to Visalia." Ace shifted his legs a little and paused for the implication of his words to take effect.

"To make it worse," he continued, "the detectives found out that George had been on the train when it was robbed. Of course, they went right after him for questioning. Both the Sontags were stopping with the Evans family in their little house on the outskirts of Visalia, and that's where the detectives went. They suspicioned that both the Sontags and Evans were mixed up in the robbery some way, so they picked up George in the front yard. Then they went up to the Evans house and knocked on the door, looking for the other two. It was Eva who came to the door; she was the daughter of Evans — sixteen years old and mighty good lookin', blond but with dark eyes. She didn't know anything about the comings and goings of her father or the Sontags, and when the detectives asked to see Sontag, Eva said he wasn't there. She later said the detectives swore at her and called her a liar, so she just ran out the back door. Her father was out back, and she told him what had happened. So Evans went in the house and got a six-shooter and took after the detectives, who got scared and ran out the front door.

"Nobody knows for sure who started it, but there was shooting and one of the deputies was injured. They hightailed it back to town, and Sontag and Evans disappeared. That's how people came to feel that they were guilty of the train robbery. But they never owned up to it; always swore it was a lie. Well, right away a hundred men spread out to look for them. They had no money or supplies, so when it got dark they came back to the house and got all the food, guns, and ammunition in the place. Guards had been left there, and they spotted 'em, and there was shooting. One guard was killed and in the excitement, Sontag and Evans got away.

"Now the manhunt was on for real. Northeast of Visalia the men borrowed a mule and a cart and worked their way up into the foothills. Once in the mountains, they left the cart and went on by trail. It was practically impossible to follow 'em because Evans had mined in the mountains and knew the trails like the back of his hand. He had friends up there, too, who were willing to hide him. The railroad and the express company offered a $10,000 reward for the train robbers' capture, and the hunt went on. The detectives dug around the Evans place and came up with $2,000 worth of Peruvian coins — or so they said. This was sure fire evidence of Sontag's and Evan's guild, but they always claimed that the detectives had planted the money there. It was used at George's trial, and they found him guilty and sent him up to Folsom for life.

"As I said, Evans had friends in the mountains. Plenty of people in that country hated the railroad and felt that Sontag and Evans were only defending their rights or had a right to get even. Seems like people are always ready to side in against a big corporation, right or wrong. I'd say this time the railroad was pretty wrong. One time Evans came down to Fresno, looked up a friend of his who happened to be a county supervisor, and said, 'Tell folks not to worry about us. We're not fighting the people of Fresno County, we're just fighting the railroad.' That's the way folks felt about it, and they were glad to see those fellows get away.

"The chase finally led to a place up in the mountains, Sampson's Flat it was, where Evans had a cabin with a fellow named Jim Young. Sontag and Evans were holed up there when a posse of ten or twelve men came in on them early one morning. It was really by accident; the posse had decided to visit old man Young to see if they could get breakfast. The old man had just stepped out to get a bucket of water, and when the leader of the posse got to the dooryard, Sontag stepped out and opened up on him. Killed him right there. Then shooting started from all sides. Another man near the first one was wounded, and he fell to his knees and begged to be spared. The outlaws agreed not to kill him, and they let him sit by the porch while the fight went on. But when they weren't looking, this man drew his gun and fired. The bullet creased Sontag's eyebrow. So Evans turned and killed the man. Now, that was a mighty foolhardy thing for that fellow to do, wasn't it?" Ace's artistry as a storyteller required a long pause at this crucial point in the narrative, and we waited while he refilled his pipe.

"Both Sontag and Evans were injured in this fight; but in the excitement, when the posse had ducked back behind some rocks to talk things over, they slipped away and escaped through a cornfield. Their trail led nowhere. And after that they were always on the move. They had three or four hiding places, and they slipped from one to another to confuse the posse. In one hideout that the posse found, they discovered bedding, provisions, and supplies, some of which had been bought before the train robbery, which led the detectives to conclude that Evans had planned the whole thing in advance and prepared ahead of time for when they would be on the run. Chris Evans was a very smart man who could always be trusted to do the unexpected, and that made him dangerous.

"Through friends, the outlaws were in contact with the Evans family all the time. Sontag and Evans wintered with a friend in the mountains and recovered from their wounds. From time to time they went down into the valley and visited with the Evans family. One day some children coming home from school reported that they had seen two ragged men at the Evans house, and word spread that Sontag and Evans were back in Visalia. The sheriff formed a posse and surrounded the home. But they were not about to go in and ask those fellows to surrender this time. Instead, they waited. It grew dark, and lights came on in the house. Then at eleven o'clock the lights went out, and all was quiet. Then all of a sudden somebody in the posse heard a noise out in the barn. The barn doors swung open, and out came a buggy with Sontag and Evans in it, whipping the horses and going for all they were worth.

They headed for the road and took off to the hills. There was shooting, but nothing came of it, only that Sontag and Evans had got away again.

"At this point the U.S. Marshals entered the picture. It was said that in the Collis train robbery some U.S. mail had been destroyed. So now the railroad detectives, the county sheriff's posse and the Federals were all after Sontag and Evans. And by now they were really closing in. They had been searching for several days, and by one Saturday night they were pretty well tuckered out. They found a vacant cabin near a landmark known as Stone Corral — an open place, very little shrubbery around it — and the posse went in there to rest over Sunday. This was just the reverse of the situation at Sampson's Flat, when the outlaws were in the cabin and the posse was on the outside.

"At just about dusk on Sunday, a lookout saw two figures coming across the meadow toward the cabin, apparently not suspicious of any danger. They came closer and closer, and finally it was established who they were. One of the posse drew a bead on Evans and fired. Evans dropped his rifle and fell. 'John — I'm gone up!' he yelled. But he was able to crawl behind a low straw pile where Sontag had taken cover. One of the posse crept out to circle behind the outlaws. He was shot in the ankle, but he continued to drag himself around behind.

"The shooting continued, and Sontag was hit in the right arm. He shifted his gun to the left hand and went on firing. But another shot caught him in the side, and he collapsed. Evans lifted himself up to look at his partner, and he was caught by a bullet in the small of his back. Sontag, in spite of his wounds, was still shooting. He was in great pain and begged for water. Evans had no water, but he crawled to where Sontag was bleeding and moaning. He said, 'I'm through, Chris.' And he begged Evans to shoot him through the head to end the pain. Evans rose just a little to see if he could ease the misery and dress Sontag's wounds a little; but as he moved, someone hit him in the right arm with a shot. Then another blast from a shotgun caught him on the side of the face and took away his right eye. And Sontag, though he was very badly wounded, could go on shooting with his left hand. Finally, night came on. There was nothing Evans could do for Sontag, and so in the dark he crawled away through the weeds, leaving a trail of blood behind. Sontag just doubled up in a little pile of straw moaning and bleeding for the rest of the night.

"The deputies could hear him there, but they waited until morning. At daybreak everything was quiet. They crept out and looked behind the straw. There lay Sontag unconscious. He had a cocked revolver in his left hand and two guns beside him. They took him down to Visalia, but he died in a few hours. Evans got away. They followed his trail of blood for quite a distance and then lost him. As it turned out, Evans dragged himself to a ranch house of some people he knew. But he was pretty weak from loss of blood and realized that he would have to turn himself in, so he sent word to the sheriff to come and get him. One condition of his surrender was that his wife was to receive part of the reward money.

"Evans' family was practically penniless. To get money to help support the family, the older daughter, Eva, went on the stage. She traveled around the country playing a part in a melodrama called *The Collis Train Robbery,* and it was supposed to depict the whole thing. This is how she raised the money for her father's defense at his trial. It was in November 1893, that the trial was held, and Evans was found guilty of murder in the first degree and sentenced to prison for life. Before he got to the penitentiary, however, he managed to escape from jail. With the help of Eva and an accomplice, who was a friend of hers, he got a gun; and after a false rumor of an expected robbery in Porterville had drawn the sheriff and his deputies away, Evans used his gun to force his escape. He and the accomplice fought their way out of town and back into the country where they hid out much as he and Sontag had done before. The chase had to begin all over again. But finally he was cornered again at his home in Visalia. This time the gunfight went on with the children right there in the house. But Evans surrendered and was sent off to prison. And that's the way my granddad told the story to me, and it's true, every word of it."

As far as Ace Morgan was concerned the story was over. The campfire had died out, the night was growing cold, and the mountains loomed higher and darker than ever. Nothing was left for us to do but crawl into our blankets and dream of the Old West, its outlaws with blazing guns and bleeding wounds, and perhaps also a blond girl who was loyal to her father.

But the story was not yet over. Subsequent inquiry brought to light a sequel that is also part of this colorful saga. In 1911 Evans was released from prison by Governor Hiram Johnson, who also fought the railroad from time to time during his career. Evans took his family to Oregon, where he died in 1917. George Sontag, the brother of the outlaw, was released from Folsom also, and immediately he set to work on a scheme to make money out of the story of the train robbery and the outlaws Sontag and Evans.

In 1914 he helped to organize a motion picture company to film a six-reel melodrama called *The Folly of a Life of Crime,* which depicted the real life story of Sontag and Evans with, of course, a few additions like a gang of outlaws to back them up. George was to play himself in the picture. The company chose Chico and Oroville as the location for the film and used local people for actors. Alex McIntyre and Jim Pickett of Chico and Al Tyrell of Durham were members of the posse. William R. Stead played the sheriff, and the part of John Sontag was played by "Hank" Pickett, both of Chico. Clyde McDonald played Evans. As old men more than fifty years later they delighted in recalling that exciting experience. "Yes," Pickett said in telling about the final battle in which Sontag was shot, "I was killed right up here in Butte Creek."

Bill Stead described the scene, "Yes, I shot him in Butte Creek with my thirty-eight revolver. But he died down there in that old African Methodist church that stood on 6th and Flume Streets in Chico. That was the place we used for the office of the sheriff. That's where the reward was posted and where the railroad detectives had their headquarters in the film." The old men explained that the director tried to make the picture as realistic as possible; he even imported some dogs from Tennessee, real prisoner-chasing bloodhounds, to track the outlaws for the camera.

There was, of course, some love interest in the show. A girl named Birdie was added to the story. Supposedly in love with Sontag, she fluttered her eyes and clasped her hands when the emotions of passion or fear were called for, and she was there to dress the wounds of the handsome young outlaw when he was down. About the love scenes Pickett recalled, "Well, I was supposed to make love to her. She was supposed to be my sweetheart, but I didn't like her much so I didn't do much about the love part."

"Oh, yes," put in Bill Stead, "that was the raggedest love-making I ever saw." But apparently it satisfied Birdie and the director. The company was three months making the picture, starting in July of 1914. It cost $136,000. The studio was in Oroville, and the outdoor locations were in Butte Creek, along Lindo Channel, and in various parts of Chico, which was supposed to represent Visalia. After a brief run, the film disappeared. Perhaps, in due time, those six reels of action-packed drama will show up again on television.

You Can't Win 'em All

Two angels sat on a cloud high over the earth and looked down and speculated on mankind. Said the Good Angel, "Man down there is by nature pretty good. Give him the good things of life and I think he will use them for the benefit of his fellow men."

The Bad Angel shook his head. "Don't you believe it," he said. "The percentage may run in your favor, but by and large I think mankind can be pretty mean. Just let me give one of them a little overdose of any one of the Seven Deadly Sins and you'll see what will happen."

"Every man," said the Good Angel, "has a certain amount of the Seven Deadly Sins in him, but given the right circumstances he will overcome them."

"I said an overdose of any one," said the Bad Angel. "You pick the man and let me give him a double-shot of — let's say, greed; that's getting a pretty good play these days." And the Bad Angel chuckled. "I'll even spot you twenty years or so on his life span. You pick your man, wind him up, and start him off in the right direction. Give him some talents to use for the benefit of mankind. And just to be fair about it, you might also give him the usual number of manly weaknesses. You fellows have a way of turning them around to your benefit in the end, anyway. After you have endowed him with talent, I'll just inject a heavy dose of greed. Then we'll turn him loose and watch the results."

The Good Angel smiled and said, "I agree. Do you see that young man down there just graduating from Harvard University? He's my man."

And the Bad Angel also smiled and said, "Agreed."

"Now you'll see that I'm right," said the Good Angel.

And the Bad Angel said, "Straighten your halo; it's on crooked. And as for your man down there — we'll see."

John Marsh graduated from Harvard University with the Class of 1823. He was intelligent and not unattractive, but he had a restlessness that drove him from place to place. For a while he was at Fort Snelling, Minnesota. Then he went to Prairie du Chien, Wisconsin. After the custom of men who lived at the edge of the wilderness, he took for himself a French and Indian girl there, a gentle creature with brown eyes and black hair. She gave him two children, both with attractive dark eyes and brown skin, a girl and a boy. For the boy, John Marsh felt a particular affection because the little fellow was marked with a deformed foot. The toes of one foot were grown together, and the boy walked with a slight shuffle or limp.

Well, John Marsh wanted more — more money to be specific — but with no particular trade and two children and their mother to support, money was not easy to acquire. Marsh grew restless, and in 1836 he left his family behind and went to California. He no doubt intended to send for them when he got situated, but he hadn't been in Los Angeles long before word reached him that the woman and the two children had died. He was embittered by the thought that if he had had money to leave for their care this might not have happened. He must get money; that became his singular life goal.

John Marsh had a talent that the people of Los Angeles desperately needed. He had a certain natural skill with sickness, had learned something of the chemistry of herbs and a little physiology and, perhaps most important, he understood the psychology of man. He knew that to a sick person, a healer is almost a god.

So John Marsh took out his diploma from Harvard, which was written in Latin, and asked the alcalde to give him a license to practice medicine. The alcalde looked at the diploma wisely and handed it to a priest from San Gabriel Mission who happened to be there. The priest studied it and then nodded approval. After all, it was a diploma. Nobody could read it, including the alcalde, and probably the priest, so why not call it a medical degree. Anyway, it looked very impressive. And thus it was that John Marsh became a doctor. He opened an office near the plaza, and the sick, the lame, the wounded of Los Angeles came to him for treatment. He took his pay in hides, which was the most negotiable medium of exchange then. The people had little else with which to pay, but it was sufficient. Dr. Marsh prospered.

And the Good Angel looked down and said, "See now. All is well."

And the Bad Angel looked off into space and said, "Wait and see."

In two years Dr. Marsh left Los Angeles. The dry, stiff, stinking hides he had collected for his fees accumulated and stacked up higher and higher out behind his office, but now he wanted more. He moved north, and in 1838 he bought a large ranch that stretched from the eastern slopes of Mount Diablo to the San Joaquin River. His cattle grazed for miles in all directions. He had trouble with

114

cattle thieves, but he fought them off. He made slaves of the Indians, but it might be said that, given the times, he thus saved them from extermination. He was a harsh master, but not cruel.

John Marsh was the only doctor in the whole region, and his services were required far and wide. However, he refused to go long distance unless he was guaranteed exorbitant fees. If he had to go to San Jose for the Castros or to Sonoma to treat one of the Vallejo children, his fee would be as much as 25 to 50 head of cattle for the call. To the poor Mexicans he gave little or no help at all.

The Marsh adobe was known to travelers far and wide, not for its hospitality but for its inhospitality and hostility. Hungry travelers needing to replenish their supplies would get from Dr. Marsh only enough to take them to the next place, and he charged outrageously for every commodity and every service. The wise traveler in the west always expected to pay more than the goods were worth, but if he had to buy from Dr. Marsh, he paid twice what anyone else would have charged. Dr. John Marsh was known — and hated — from one end of California to the other. People stayed out of his way whenever they could. As the years went by, he grew greedier, richer and more despised.

"Well, how are things going?" asked the Bad Angel.

"Not too well at the moment," admitted the Good Angel. "I think something is missing, but I can't quite put my finger on it." And the Good Angel squirmed a little to adjust a misplaced feather in his wing.

"Here, let me help you with that," said the Bad Angel. "Looks like you will be molting a little early again this year. You worry too much."

"As I was saying," said the Good Angel, "something is missing. This experiment isn't turning out quite the way I had expected. I think I'll try a little dash of love; it might work better this time"

In 1847 an acquaintance wrote to Dr. Marsh from one of the hot springs in Napa Valley; he encouraged Marsh to come to the valley to find a wife, especially recommending "two young ladies who are well worth the ride to see. In fact, there are a number of ladies, including several long-built widows, in the fertile valley of Napa." But Marsh was not interested. In 1849 he was busy selling beef to the hungry miners on the Yuba and American Rivers. He was growing rich.

However, in 1850 he met a girl from Massachusetts. She was attractive, intelligent, educated, and thrilled with the adventure of the new land in California. It was as if she had been sent by providence to step into the life of John Marsh and draw him out of himself.

Abby Tuck was a special kind of girl, and John Marsh knew it. In 1851 they were married. They lived in the old adobe which the Indians had built for Marsh, but they planned something better. The miserly doctor grew more generous, even reaching into his secret hoard for money to pay an architect to design what was to be one of the finest mansions in California. Work on the mansion was barely started when a daughter, Alice, was born to the Marshes. The mother was never well after that, and life at the adobe was hard. In 1855, before the big mansion was finished, Abby died.

The test was too great for Dr. Marsh to endure. He quickly returned to his miserly ways, and other troubles came upon him. Squatters settled on his land, thieves drove his cattle away, and a deadly feud with one of his neighbors made life more miserable than ever for the unhappy man. He trusted no one. His fight now was to keep what he had accumulated; it became his life's obsession.

The Good Angel was distressed. "I'm afraid we didn't give love quite enough time," he said. "He was showing so much improvement I'm afraid I became a little too optimistic."

"Your halo is tilting again," said the Bad Angel. "I wouldn't want you to call a foul on the experiment now. Tell you what I'll do. I'll give you one more chance to prove that good can triumph over man's greed. I'll spot you to a small miracle — nothing spectacular, you understand. We mustn't pull anything that will upset the Master Plan. But you might think of something that will throw a little help and compassion and human sympathy his way."

"I'll try," said the Good Angel.

The big house was finished in 1856. With only the child Alice and a few Indian servants to keep him company, Dr. John Marsh lived alone. The great mansion was not even properly furnished. Late one night, as he was dozing in his chair, Marsh was startled by the sudden appearance of a stranger who had just walked into the room. The seedy, tired, hungry looking man was in need of food and rest, but, as always, Marsh was inhospitable. He ordered the stranger out of the house and told him to leave the ranch.

"But, Sir, I'm so tired. I've lost my way — and when I saw your light here, I thought . . ."

"Have you any money?" Marsh demanded.

"No, Sir."

"Well, a man has no business traveling here afoot and without money." But the stranger wouldn't leave, and finally John Marsh consented to let him stay the night. He was not, however, offered any food nor a bed, only a place to rest by the fire.

After a time, Marsh asked, "Where are you from?"

"San Francisco — just out from the States."

"What state?"

"Illinois." The stranger didn't notice that his host was becoming interested.

"What is your name?"

"Marsh," the young man answered.

"Marsh? Marsh! From Illinois? Where were you born?"

"Wisconsin. My father was an educated man who came out west. My mother died when I was a boy, and I was raised by some kindly people." The young man had dark skin and dark eyes.

"What are you here for?" Dr. Marsh shouted.

"Ever since my mother and little sister died, I've wanted to find my father. I think he must be a great and successful man out west here somewhere. I was heading for the San Joaquin, but I got lost. Tomorrow I'll be on my way again."

Dr. Marsh was pacing the floor. "Take off your boot!" he ordered. The visitor, startled by the request, only stared at the excited old man. He was not sure he understood. "I said take off your boot." With some hesitation, the astonished man complied. "Now your stocking." In embarrassment the traveler showed his foot. The toes were grown together. And Dr. Marsh then knew the young man was his son. It was a small miracle that the young man should find his father in this way and be recognized. Explanations revealed that the mother and daughter had died, but the son had lived. All his life he had dreamed of the day when he would be a man and could go west to find his father, whom he had grown to idealize with all the great qualities of a good and successful man.

Charles Marsh stayed with his father at the ranch. For a while the young man was treated as a son, and the old doctor seemed happy. But gradually the filial privileges were withdrawn, the money was doled out in pennies, and in a few months the young man was laboring among the Indians, he the slave and Dr. Marsh the master.

The Bad Angel polished his fingernail with a feather. "You give up?" he asked.

"Yes," said the Good Angel. "I suppose we might as well close out the experiment. I'll give up — but only on this one."

"Well," said the Bad Angel, "You can't win 'em all."

So in the fall of 1856, while traveling in his buggy from his ranch to Martinez, Dr. Marsh was held up and murdered by two of his vaqueros, who thought he was carrying $5,000 in gold. The money was not there. Marsh's son, Charles, was declared legitimate by the courts and he shared the inheritance with his half-sister, Alice. After that, the grand old mansion stood neglected for many years, like a somber reminder of an unhappy life ruined by selfishness and greed. It is now a historical monument.

Lynching at Lookout Bridge

The town was old, and withered, and dying. The one street that threaded the town together was swept clean by that steady, dry plateau wind of Northern California. The old grocery store with its high, square board front; the remains of a once-shaded blacksmith shop, now turned into a makeshift garage; the beer parlor and sporting goods emporium that had once been a saloon; and the four or five skeletons of old houses. With bare driveways and front paths that still clung to the road like bony fingers — this was the town of Lookout. The boards of what had once been a short raised sidewalk in front of the store had shrunk, and the paint — where there had been paint on the buildings — had dried, and curled and peeled off, and the wood sidewalls had that pale, crisp, sun-bleached look. It was a town fighting against death and decay.

At the end of the town a single crossroad led to the cemetery. It was surprisingly well-kept and green, that cemetery, the greenest part of town, as if its role had somehow been reversed and here lay the life of the village. Green, that is, except for one spot in the extreme southwest corner where the Russian thistle and the cheat grass grew unmolested. Here was a single grave marked by a single wooden marker which, until recent years, bore only one name "Hall." In this lonesome grave lay the bodies of five men.

The people of Bieber and Adin and Alturas still don't talk much about these five men. Nobody cares to remember. Somewhere in Alturas, where the trial was held, there's a letter that is yet to be opened, which may tell the true story. It was written by a member of the jury, but it cannot be opened until the last man who remains of that conscience-stricken jury has died.

Most of the story had gradually come out, at least as the folk remember it — an eighty-year-old woman, who lay in her last sickness in an Alturas hospital; a Beiber woman whose father had lived in Lookout at the time; a man of importance in the county whose boyhood memories were still vivid; and the "old-timer" who, like the ancient mariner, lived it again and again and who swore with the conviction of one who could not be contradicted that, "Of all the fellers that took part in that thing — I can tell you — Hell overtook them, ever' one of 'em."

Calvin Hall had been a soldier at Fort Crook in 1861. He had taken a friendly interest in the Indians, and when left the Army he married an Indian girl and they had moved to Lookout. It was then a rough and ready outpost town for miners and ranchers. Hall had settled on a few acres up in a little draw call Gouger's Neck, and there he and his Indian wife raised a family. The years went by and Calvin Hall's boys came to suffer the hatred toward half-breeds so common in the West. They struck back in the only way they knew, and word got around that they were a bad lot. People laid the blame on them for a series of petty thefts like raiding chicken coops, stealing harnesses, making away with calves and, in general, trespassing on the sacred property of other ranchers

After a while the Hall ranch was known as a stopping place for renegades — desperate men on the run from sheriffs, or lesser offenders who needed a place to hide out until their crimes were forgotten in the excitement of newer offenses against the peace and security of Northern California.

"An' that ain't all," a man called Shorty was heard to say one day to his fellow loungers in the country store."That ain't all." And with a sarcastic twinkle in his eye: "Them Calvin Hall scum raises the best tomaters in the valley, an' they're a-sellin' 'em cheaper'n ever' body else. An' that ain't just right. I ever said, the Halls has got to go!"

Matters went from bad to worse until the summer of 1901. Old Calvin Hall was in his 70s then. His boys, Frank and Jim, were about grown, and the youngest boy was past thirteen. There was a girl, too, about middlin' size. And at this time, staying with them was a questionable character named Dan Yantes. He had been a real bad man sometime, somewhere, and his temporary abode with the Halls only served to kindle the smoldering fires of community indignation. One by one the other citizens of Lookout came around to Shorty's insistent opinion that the Halls must go, one way or another.

Finally, in May of 1901, Frank and Jim Hall and Dan Yantes were arrested for stealing. They were locked in the makeshift jail and when old Calvin Hall and his youngest boy came down to investigate, they were thrown in jail with the others.

"I don't know about this, boys," said the worried town marshal."You ain't got no evidence that'll stick in court."

Doubt, perplexity, and disappointment spread over the faces of Lookout's citizens.

"You just let me on the jury, and I'll hang it on em," muttered a big man wearing a calf-skin vest. He had forgotten the fact that he also was one of the injured parties and was to be a complaining witness.

"It ain't no jury business," the marshal said. "This won't get past the judge, even."

"Can't let 'em go now," Shorty put in. "You let 'em go now, you're just askin' fer trouble. They'll take it out on you. You've got 'em now. They got it comin' and you'll never get 'em again like you got 'em now. I say let's get a rope!"

"I got a rope. I got plenty of rope," said a man with a big nose and a broad mustache.

"An' I say let's take 'em," Shorty said, with rising emotion.

The talk spread, and the smoldering anger leaped into flame. Perplexity and doubt gave way to conviction, purpose, and action. Seven ropes were brought out, five for the men in the jail, and two for the mother and daughter who were lurking somewhere on the outskirts of town. The marshal knew in his heart that he couldn't be a party to such an outrage, not and remain faithful to his office. But when it was pointed out that "what he didn't know couldn't hurt him," he agreed to a plan that would subject his conscience only to the pangs of an unfortunate oversight. He would forget and leave the jail unguarded when he went out for supper. After all, a marshal has to eat his supper.

That night the moon shone big and round and golden over the wide valley. The two women, mother and daughter, sensing trouble, hid behind some sagebrush on a hill nearby, watching the moon-drenched town and the shadows moving up and down the street. At the agreed moment, the marshal left the jail, stepped up on the boardwalk in front of the hotel, and lighted his cigar. This was the signal. He turned and went in to supper, and the waiting mob rushed in to have its feast. The five men were dragged out of jail and up the street to the high log bridge that stretched across the little river at the edge of town.

The ropes were tied at one end to the poles at the top of the bridge. At the other end were hangman's nooses. The two women were forgotten in the excitement, and they crouched on the hillside nearby, watching. Old Calvin Hall, seventy, tired and spent, had lived his life. There wasn't enough left to fight for. The noose was fixed, and he was dropped over the bridge. Frank had started to fight, but a vicious blow to the chin by the big man with the calf-skin vest had brought the sweet blessing of unconsciousness, and he went over without knowing. Jim Hall was paralyzed with terror. Mumbling incoherent words and trembling with the sick weakness of his fear, he was lifted over and dropped. Dan Yantes, for some strange reason, submitted in sullen resignation. Perhaps he knew, in his heart, that this was his appointed destiny and the time had now come.

But it was the young boy, the thirteen-year-old, big for his age and full of life, who fought back. He screamed and cursed. He bit at the hands that clutched him. He swung his fists wildly and grabbed at the throat of the man with the big nose. He kicked another man in the stomach so hard the man turned sick. But after a terrific struggle he, too, was dropped from the bridge. And the man named Shorty, who had stood back at the edge of the bridge during these latter proceedings, spat in the water that flowed quietly under the bridge.

The moon shone full and rich and almost warm on the little town that night. And as the shadows of the now quiet citizens moved slowly back into town, to linger in little groups and clusters by the hotel, near the blacksmith shop or at the edge of the board sidewalk, there were five other shadows that twisted and swung in the moonlight. The river, like a ribbon of glancing blue light, flowed slowly under the bridge, and a large cloud slid over the moon and spread its broad shadow over the town of Lookout.

The next day the Indian woman and her daughter were allowed to come into town and take away the bodies of their men. How the men were buried, and by whom, is not remembered. Then the women took out their old round-topped tin-covered trunk, packed it, loaded it into the wagon, and drove to Alturas, where, during the years that followed, the mother worked at cleaning houses for one family after another until she died. What became of the girl no one seems to know.

Some of the men who were involved in the affair were brought to trial. Local folk came to listen to the testimony, and although they seemed to consider it seriously, they but didn't say much. The jury brought in a verdict of "Not Guilty," and the accused men went their way. Some of them left the country and were never heard of again. But some of them stayed, and as the years passed, their guilt etched itself on their faces.

The folk in those towns have come to know what became of the men who did this thing. Ask them, and they'll tell you — if they feel like talking about it. They say that all these men came to a tragic or evil end. One walked in front of a train, and it wasn't exactly an accident. One died of cancer of the throat, right where an imaginary noose might have gone, or the hand of a wretched boy might have clutched. One died from a rotting of the stomach just as if he had been kicked there. And the folk will tell you, "Hell overtook every one of 'em." Even the bridge caught fire one night and burned away.

And if you visit that little cemetery, in the town of Lookout, you will find that time has brought at least one change to that desolate corner where the lone grave lies. Someone — the sexton can't remember who — has placed a neat, thin stone slab there. It bears the simple inscription: "Calvin Hall, Sergeant, 2nd U.S. Cavalry."

But the final touch of irony is that when Calvin Hall was a soldier at Fort Crook in 1861 he kept a journal in which he described the way of life among the Indians as he knew them. His observations were so accurate and his accounts were written with such clear, objective, scientific detail, that today he is quoted by scholars as one of the best authorities on the Indians of that region. He has left a gift to science that will make his name immortal, and Calvin Hall will have the respect of men who will never know the name of the man with the calf-skin vest, the man with the big nose, or the man called Shorty.

High Spirits

It had been a pleasant afternoon, and the four old men who sat in the cool shade of the city square were at peace with the world. As had been their custom for several years, on the long, warm summer days they would come together as if by appointment, drawn into a natural fellowship by their advancing age and the frustrating awareness of their general obsolescence in the community. As usual, they had arranged the two park benches to avoid the direct heat of the sun and had relaxed into the routine review of current events. This part of the ritual having been accomplished, they drifted comfortably into quiet meditation or casual references to the moving scene on the sidewalks of the various business establishments around the outside of the square.

A man and a woman were having an argument over by the courthouse corner, but it didn't seem important enough to try to listen to. A dog made his way across the square, and the old men watched him in silence as he trotted from bush to bush. His manifestations of doghood were accepted by these four ancient philosophers as being right and proper; no comment was necessary. A woman was pushing her half-nude infant in a small cart along the sidewalk. She stopped in front of the drug store, left the child in the shade of the doorway, and disappeared inside. After a while she came out, put a small package in the cart beside the baby, and went on to the corner. Another woman came out of Elmer's Cafe and walked briskly along, not bothering to glance at the elegant merchandise in the store windows.

"There goes that waitress off shift again," remarked one of the four watchers.

"Mighty fine figure of a woman," said the second watcher, a frail old man with white hair and whiskers.

"Want to bet she'll do it again?" the third put in quickly. But no one responded to the offer. The waitress walked halfway down the block, paused slightly, and entered the doorway under a sign that said, "Elite Bar."

"Well, she's done it again," said the first man.

"Now, Ace, you never did think she wouldn't, did you?" responded the one who had offered the bet that she would. "After a hard day's work in there for Elmer, that girl has just got to have a drink before she goes on home. Does it every time."

"Yeah," said the man called Ace. His tone was one of complete approval. He was in his eighties now, and his wife had been dead for six years; he knew about the tensions of women and their need to find some means of relaxing from a hard day's work. "It won't do her no harm to take a little nip. Might get her home that much easier."

"Mighty fine lookin' woman," repeated the second old man, he with the white hair and beard. He had not strayed from that thought since she had first appeared. The fourth old man was looking, but he said nothing.

"Well," my old lady was a fine lookin' woman, too," said Ace. "But she shore wasn't easy to live with. Sometimes, that is."

"She wear the britches in your house?" asked the third man, a lean, bald headed, leather faced individual, whose wife was still very much alive.

"Not exactly. Not all the time. But she could be stubborn and cantankerous sometimes." Old Ace had good memories of his wife, but he also knew that his listeners expected an honest and realistic answer. His reminiscences frequently blossomed into full grown stories, listened to and appreciated by one and all, and he prided himself in his reputation for faithfulness to the subject. "But she shore could be contrary," Ace went on. "Why, that woman was so contrary, if she was to drown in the river she'd float upstream."

"You look like you done pretty well," said the leather faced man. "She must not of been such a trial to you."

"Well, one thing, she didn't drink."

Ace took off his well-worn hat and fanned his face and neck. "That waitress puts me in mind of a story that old Doc Shipley used to tell around here. You remember Doc. He was the best baby catcher this town had for about forty years." They all remembered Doc Shipley.

"Old Doc used to tell one — I don't know where he got it; maybe heard it from some of the family. They still live around here. Anyway he told it for the truth, and I've heard tell that some folks admit it." Old Ace was settling into a yarn, and his companions waited with respect and anticipation.

"It seems that this old couple lived on their farm several miles out west of Healdsburg — five, six, maybe seven miles. I never did get a location on the place exactly. The way Doc told it, it was back in the 1860s, but that would have been more than a hundred years ago. It may not have been that far back. Anyhow, this old couple used to fight a lot. They could get up an argument on just about everything. Come Monday morning they'd start out. Who was to carry in the wood? Who was to claim the egg money? What was to be for supper? Things like that. This would go on, the battle getting worse and worse, until Saturday. They were about the fightin'est pair to ever enjoy marital bliss.

"But on one thing these old coots could agree. Most of the time, that is. They could always settle every argument with a good stiff toddy. Come Saturday night they would open the jug together and spend a joyful evening like a couple of old sailors, drinking and pounding the table and laughing at each other's cleveralities. Regular as the Saturday night bath, they'd patch everything up over that joy juice. Then they'd spend Sunday resting up, and on Monday morning they were ready to start fightin' all over again.

"It seems that every Saturday afternoon the old man would come to town for the mail and a few supplies. Then he'd go back and do the chores, and after supper that's when he would bring out the keg and they would settle down to serious drinkin' and peace makin'. The trouble was that pretty soon the old man noticed that the old woman was hitting the keg while he was off to town. She couldn't wait, her thirst was that strong.

"Well, this wasn't fair. She wasn't playin' the game strictly according to Hoyle. He ordered her to leave the liquor alone while he was away. She right out and refused. He tried to convince her by various methods that it was unladylike to drink alone. But she was like a breachy cow that had found a hole in the fence, and she wouldn't stop.

"So one Saturday he took the keg out and hid it in the haystack before he went off to town. When he came home that night he found the old lady well along toward jubilation just the same. She had found the jug of oh-be-joyful and was already far ahead of him in the benefit of its potent virtue. The next week he hid the keg in the smoke house under some slabs of bacon. That evening it was the same story. She had found it and the nose paint was already on. She could beat him to the draw every time.

"Week after week the same thing would happen. No matter where he hid the stuff, the old woman would always smell it out. It got to be a contest between them. It was like a challenge to bring out the best in him, and he studied on it for a long time. Finally one day he got an inspiration. He was out in the yard thinking about where to hide it, and he happened to look up into a big live oak tree that they had out back there. That's when his master scheme came to him in a flash. That tree was the answer to his problem. Why try to hide the liquor at all? He would swing his keg of precious juice on a limb high up in that tree, out of reach. She would be able to see it there, but she couldn't climb that tree to get at it. There it would hang and it wouldn't matter how thirsty she got; she wouldn't be able to touch it till he got home.

"So the very next Saturday before he started off to town, he fixed it up just right. He got a ladder and a set of blocks and tackle, and he swung the five-gallon keg some thirty feet off the ground to a limb of that tree. 'Now,' says he to himself, 'when I come home tonight, old girl, you'll be as sober as a judge.' And he went to town feeling pretty good about it. He told it around town about how he finally out-smarted the old woman, and the boys all got a big laugh out of it. He stayed a little later than usual that day, and he didn't get home until about sundown.

"Well, when he got home he found his dear spouse out in the yard under the tree. She was flat on the ground and pickled to the gills. He looked up into the tree. There hung the keg exactly where he had put it. Straight down under that suspended keg was the old family wash tub. And in the tub was what was left of his good liquor.

"It didn't take him long to figure out what had happened. His honey had spied the keg hanging there out of reach, just as he thought she would, and with no way to get at it. She had brought out the old wooden wash tub and put it on the ground right under it. She was not about to be cheated no matter what.

"She went back into the house and brought out the old eight-square squirrel rifle that he called 'Meat-in-the-pot,' that they had brought across the plains from Missouri. Well, she was a crack shot, and she took good aim. She shot a hole right into the bottom of that keg. The fire water squirted out of the hole and into the waiting tub below. And that's how she spited her husband, and I guess you'd have to admit that she won that battle of wits.

"He seemed to surrender after that. Like the old keg with the hole in it, the spirit had somehow gone out of him. I guess he never again tried to plague the old woman. He even went so far as to make some adjustments to accommodate her. The cost of the liquor was getting a little out of hand, so he bought up some old moldy grain that came on the market, and he made himself a little still, and he did enough moonshining on the side to keep the two of them well supplied.

"According to old Doc Shipley, they had many a merry fight after that, and afterwards they always had a joyful peace conference."

Some time after Ace had finished his story and appropriate comments had been pronounced on it, the waitress came out of the bar and headed off down the street. The four old men watched her go.

"Mighty fine figure of a woman," said one of them, with a note of distant wistfulness in his voice. She turned the corner and disappeared from sight.

Ishi – the Man

Threatened with extinction, either from the scientific genius of an enemy or by our own cancerous or ozone-depleting waste and pollution, we might well speculate in our fantasies what we could do if the end of our civilization and our race should come. When one imagines death, the concept can reach to everyone except himself. It is natural, therefore, for the dreamer to imagine that he and perhaps a few of his friends are the last of his civilization, the final handful of survivors upon whom the divine gift of Eden is bestowed and from whose loins a new race will spring. Such speculation leads inevitably to certain questions which always must accommodate two controlling forces: choice and necessity. If an enemy from another continent or another planet conquered us, would we retreat to some mountain hideaway to fight on like the guerillas of past wars even to the point of ultimate victory or extinction? What would we try to save of our present culture? What scientific formulas? What skills? What books? What music or art? Or would we succumb to the hopeless loneliness of it and forget and wander and die?

These questions are not exclusively the concern of science fiction or personal fantasy. At least once this has actually happened. Here in our western land, in the memory of man, in one microcosmic instance, an enemy came, a culture was destroyed, the people died, and finally that ultimate single survivor stood alone. The story has been told many times but never more beautifully than by Mrs. Theodora Kroeber in her book, *Ishi — in Two Worlds*. It is a chronicle of survival and adaptation against the insuperable odds of an ultimate force. What we might fear in our own fantasies was, for Ishi, very real. The analogy is unmistakable to one who has walked, as I have, in the wild, desolate, hostile country that was Ishi's. I have felt the awful loneliness of this vast wilderness; I have seen the cave where many of his helpless people were massacred and I have touched the dust of their bones; I have spread over my shoulders the fur robe that Ishi once wore when he was a wild man, the last of his race; and I have talked with people who knew him and found in him a tender human, and in many ways a very wise man.

For most people the story begins at a point near the end, the climax really, of a long and bitter and lonely fight against overwhelming odds for survival. It was early in the morning of August 28, 1911. Some people coming to work were attracted by the noisy barking of dogs at a slaughterhouse near Oroville. An attendant went out to investigate and, over in a corner of the corral fence, found a strange creature huddled in fear and shaking as if from the cold. He wore only a ragged sack-like wrap. He was weak and thin, half-starved, and his hair was cropped short with dirt and ashes smeared on his head. No doubt he expected to be killed immediately, for all he had known from the white men throughout his life was hostility, hatred, and death. But to his surprise he was taken in and treated with kindness, given some tobacco, and offered food. The sheriff was called, and the sorry creature was taken to the Butte County jail for safekeeping.

He could not understand English or Spanish. Some Indians were called in, but they could not communicate with him either. Here was truly a wild man, as if he had just stepped out of a cave from prehistoric times. He had committed no crime and no one came to identify or claim him, so the sheriff had to decide what to do with him. The story soon reached the newspapers, and people came from everywhere to stare at the Indian. This wild man of Oroville quickly became a national sensation, and writers told the world that a genuine stone-age man had been found. One enterprising promoter with an eye toward making himself richer even tried to persuade the sheriff to put the poor fellow in his custody so he could take him around the country and exhibit him in sideshows.

About this time Professors Kroeber and Waterman of the Anthropology Department at the University of California asked the sheriff to hold the wild man for scientific study. Waterman was an expert on Indian languages, and he came to Oroville and attempted to talk with the Indian. He tried out several word lists from the languages of the Indian tribes of the area, but nothing seemed to make sense to the captive. Finally, the Indian seemed to recognize one or two words from a dialect of the Yana, who had once occupied the mountains east of Redding. The Yana were almost extinct, but their language was known. The Yahi, their old neighbors and relatives to the south, were assumed to be completely extinct and their language was lost. But with only a word or two to establish the first link, it was ascertained that this wild man was one of the Yahi.

Professor Waterman took the Indian to the University of California Museum of Anthropology, which was in San Francisco at that time, and bit by bit they reconstructed the language of the Yahi, the lost tribe. This human museum piece was given a name, but it was not his real one. That name he never revealed. *Ishi* was the Yahi word which meant simply "man," so the man was called

Ishi. The name satisfied him, and as time went on he even came to be called Mr. Ishi.

His movement from the stone age to modern civilization was perhaps the greatest step any man has ever been called upon to make. To show how great that adjustment must have been, let's go back and pick up the story of his people.

• • •

In 1850, about ten years before Ishi was born, the Yana and Yahi occupied 2,000 to 2,400 square miles of territory in the foothills east and south of Redding. By 1872, when Ishi was about ten years old, there were none of his Yahi people known to be left alive, and very few of the Yana. Approximately three to four thousand Indians had been made slaves in California from 1852 to 1867. Disease and mass murder had almost put an end to those that remained. The decade of the 1860s was a period of white encroachment and Indian withdrawal, raids of extermination, concealment and starvation. In the early 1870s the clash between the Indians and the whites reached its final stage, and the few who remained of Ishi's people went into hiding. For about twenty-two years, from 1872 to 1894, Ishi's people lived in such complete secrecy, the whites did not even suspect that they existed.

Carefully, they avoided the white man's town and cabin. Their camps were hidden and their storage shelters were disguised. Not a footprint, not a telltale bit of ash or wisp of smoke from a fire was seen; not a single broken arrowshaft or a lost spearpoint was found. They traveled sometimes for long distances by leaping from boulder to boulder, their bare feet leaving no print. Or they walked in streambeds, making the water their pathway and leaving no trail. Each footprint on the ground was covered with leaves and obliterated. Their paths went under the heavy chaparral, not through it, and they had to crawl along those places on all fours. A cow could not follow such trails. Even the deer could not go where these people picked their way. If a branch was in the way, it was carefully bent back, and when it had to be cut, it was worn through with a crude tool made from a splintered rock. It was a slow but silent process. They never chopped, the sound of chopping being the unmistakable announcement of human presence. They kept their fires small and covered the site of every campfire with broken rock as soon as the fire went out.

They harpooned fish or caught them in nets. They used the bow and arrow and caught small game with snares. These were all silent ways of getting food. In the autumn they would gather acorns for grinding into meal. In the spring they ate the green wild clover, and in the summer they dug for bulbs and roots. These, too, were silent ways. Yet, through these hidden years of death-in-life, they kept their will to survive long after all hope of survival had vanished. We might well wonder where they got their inner strength for the long endurance, whence came their courage and their faith.

By 1894 it was suspected that a few Indians were living in those hills, but no one knew for sure. By this time the people of Ishi had been reduced to only five persons: Ishi, his sister, his aged mother, an old man, and another young man. But the young man died, leaving Ishi and his sister to take care of the two old people.

In 1908 Ishi's family were seen. By chance, a party of surveyors stumbled upon one of the Indians' secret camps. The old man and the sister ran away, and the old mother was found lying under some skins, apparently in great pain. The surveyors ransacked the camp and took everything they could find. There was a fire drill and the usual Yahi cooking utensils; there were arrow-flaking tools, a deer snare, bow, arrows, quivers, a two-pronged spear, baskets, moccasins, tanned hides, and a fur robe made from wildcat pelts. All these things the surveyors took away as trophies, leaving the Indians without any means of livelihood.

When Ishi came back to the camp he found his mother, but the other two were gone. He never saw his sister or the old man again. He carried his mother to a new place of safety and looked after her as best he could until she died. It is likely that she had died just before he came in to surrender at the Oroville slaughterhouse in 1911, for he had cut his hair short, which was his people's sign of mourning. But Ishi would never say. In his culture, it was wrong to speak of the dead.

The ordeal of adjustment was great, but apparently civilization was not unpleasant for Ishi. He was protected from the curious crowds until he was ready to meet people. He was given his own living quarters at the museum and was allowed to work around the place to contribute to his keep. He even received a small monthly wage, which was converted into half-dollar pieces because that was what he wanted, and part of these he saved each month and put away for safekeeping. Among his close friends he was cheerful, and eventually he took obvious pride in demonstrating the skills of his people — the chipping of arrowheads, the use of the bow, the making of nets, and, of course, the secrets of his language.

On one occasion he led a party of scientists back into his wild mountain country, but he did not enjoy the rigors of camping out; he had entered the Twentieth Century and wanted nothing more to do with the primitive existence he had left behind.

Mrs. Delila Gifford, whose husband was the curator of the museum, remembers having had Ishi as a house guest many times, and always he was neat, clean, orderly, and polite. He quickly learned proper table manners, though many white man customs did not make much sense. He was friendly but never forward. He never used words until he was sure of their meaning. He never talked of the dead, and he never revealed his personal name; these were sacred things that required respect.

Ishi was not surprised that there were such things as railway trains, but he marveled that man could make them respond to his will. He was not impressed by the tall buildings in San Francisco, but he never ceased to be intrigued by the fact that a window shade would go up and down at man's bidding. He was not particularly entertained by a vaudeville show, but he never lost interest in the audience and their reactions. He did not seem to think it strange that man could accumulate wealth — his own half-dollar pieces were piling up in the safe — but was impressed by the fact that man could put it to work or spend it or save it as he pleased. He was not surprised that there were more people in the city than anyone could comprehend, but he was awed and a little frightened when so many of them could be at ease in such close quarters with one another. As Ishi saw our civilization, he was not particularly impressed by the great things that man could create, but he marveled at man's apparent ability to control what he had created and wondered what man would do if the time ever came when he could not control these things.

On March 25, 1916, about five years after Ishi came into our age, he sickened and died of tuberculosis. His passing was deeply mourned by his friends at the University. One of them wrote: "And so, stoic and unafraid, departed the last wild Indian of America. He closes a chapter in history. He looked upon us as sophisticated children — smart, but not wise. He knew many things, and much that is false. He knew nature, which is always true. His were the qualities of character that last forever. He was kind, he had courage and self-restraint, and though all had been taken from him, there was no bitterness in his heart. His soul was that of a child, his mind that of a philosopher."

There was much in Ishi's life that was truly heroic, and there was simplicity in his death. His last words were what he had often said to his friends: "You stay; I go."

Educational Enhancements

Idea #1 — Here's an entertaining and educational way to enjoy reading Hector Lee's stories and at the same time learn more about California geography and history.

The *20 Tales of California Locations Chart* at the back of this book shows over 100 places where action took place. Some stories involve several places and some places appear in more than one story.

Here's one suggested activity:

For a family outing or a group field trip, visit one or more of the places and look for locations mentioned in the stories and try to visualize the action that took place long ago in Hector Lee's stories.

Preparation:
◊ First read the stories together at home, in class, or in your group
◊ Decide which stories you want to research
◊ Refer to a map of California and appoint one person (or a team) to be the map location spotter
◊ Read the selected stories again. As a place is mentioned in the story, the map location spotter points out and/or highlights each place on the map
◊ Then plan your itinerary and make travel arrangements.

Benefits include the following:
(1) reading for fun and information
(2) learning California geography
(3) learning California history and/or folklore
(4) organizing a trip or outing
(5) teamwork
(6) fresh air adventure and fun

Idea #2 — Here's a way to encourage creative writing and cross-generational communication. Research and write a tale of California history or folklore and send it to Rayve Productions for possible inclusion in a subsequent edition of *More Tales of California.* Write to POB 726, Windsor CA 95492 for a copy of Rayve Productions writers guidelines.

◊ Think of someone who may know a story about an event in California history. Consider family members, friends, church members, community leaders, etc.

◊ Ask the person if you may interview him or her to understand the details of the story.

◊ Write down questions to ask:
> **Who** was the story about?
> **What** happened in the story? What makes it exciting and interesting?
> **When** did the story happen?
> **Where** did the story take place?
> **Why** did the events in the story occur?

◊ Research background information at the library, on the internet, etc.

◊ Write the story.

◊ Proofread the story. Spellcheck it. Read it again and edit it mercilessly. Have some friends read the story and critique it. Edit it again.

Questions & Activities

LAST TRAIN FROM LUFFENHOLTZ

1. List six to ten characteristics of John Atwell and Charlie DuVander. (e.g, courageous, skilled) Can you name a modern hero with these same qualities? Describe him or her.

2. Why do you think Atwell and DuVander risked their lives to save the people of Luffenholtz? Compare your list with classmates'.

3. Imagine you are one of the townspeople trapped by the fire. Describe your feelings and thoughts in story, poem, or song.

4. Write a front page newspaper article about the Luffenholtz fire.

5. Why do you think the citizens of Luffenholtz never returned to rebuild the town? Consider social and economic reasons.

6. Create a picture, mobile or diorama illustrating the town of Luffenholtz and/or its devastating fire.

FATHER FLORIAN'S SECRET

1. Why did the men of Sawyer's Bar feel they needed a "man of God" in town? What did they expect he would do for them? Did he satisfy their expectations?

2. Develop a male character who might have lived in a mining camp, and describe one day in his life from sunrise to sunset (or beyond).

3. Why do you think Father Florian kept his painting a secret? Write a fictional short story about the origin of the painting.

4. Considering Father Florian's talents, what sort of home and education do you think he had.

5. Other than miners, who else might have lived in a mining camp? Were they important to the community? Why or why not?

141

THE RUSSIAN AND THE LADY

1. Compare Concepcion Arguello's life to that of a modern girl. How are they similar? How are they different?

2. Why were the Mexicans and Russians fearful of one another? Describe an international situation today this is similar.

3. Would you enjoy having Concha Arguello or Count Nicolai as a friend? Why? Why not?

4. After Count Niolai returned to Russia, why do you think he or his family did not contact Concepcion? Give specific reasons.

5. Imagine you are Concepcion and write a poem or letter to Nicolai.

6. You are Count Niloai preparing to return to Alaska. What preparations must you make? What possible hazards will you face?

HATFIELD THE RAINMAKER

1. Describe your (or your parents' or grandparents') most dramatic weather experience. How did it change everyday life?

2. Imagine you are a reporter and interview Charley Hatfield or a member of the city council. Write the story for newspaper or TV.

3. If Charley Hatfield and the City of San Diego had negotiated a contract, briefly describe what items it should have emphasized.

4. If you could design a machine to control the weather, how would you use it? What power would it give you?

5. List six to ten modern methods for managing rain and drought problems (e.g., dams, low-flush toilets). Can you think of other methods not yet tried?

6. Describe life as you imagine it durng San Diego's drought -- the sights, sounds, smells and methods people used to survive.

142

DIAMONDS IN THE BIG ROCK CANDY MOUNTAINS

1. What personal characteristics helped make Mr. Arnold and Mr. Slack successful swindlers?

2. Why were sophisticated bankers, geologists, investors and diamond experts fooled by Arnold and Slack?

3. Write a story segment or movie scene describing how Arnold and Slack came up with their grand scheme.

4. Imagine you are the owner of an 1870s gold mine. Design an ad to 1) sell your gold or 2) recruit mine workers.

5. If you could go back in time to 1870s San Francisco, what character would you choose to be. Why? Describe your life.

6. If you lived in the 1870s and became wealthy mining gold or diamonds, how would spend or use your riches?

BLACK BART, SHOTGUN POET

1. Charles E. Boles, alias Black Bart, was from San Francisco. Why do you think he robbed stagecoaches in remote areas?

2. Design a "WANTED" poster that is sure to get attention.

3. Imagine you are a passenger in a stagecoach stopped by Black Bart. Describe your thoughts and feelings. (Two or more students can work on this and, using chairs, re-enact the scene for the class.)

4. Adopting Black Bart's style and meter, write a poem or two about everyday events in your life.

5. Why do you think Jimmie Rollerie shot at Black Bart? What was he thinking? Was he wise? What other action could he have taken?

6. Other than robbers, what other dangers might a stagecoach driver have encountered? Compare your list with classmates.

ONCE UPON A WINTER NIGHT

1. Would you enjoy having the Turners for neighbors? What do you like most about them? What least?

2. Imagine you are Maggie Turner and write journal entries for spring, summer, fall and winter. Be sure to describe your feelings.

3. List or draw a picture of each item the Turners needed to survive in the wilderness. Where or how would they get these things?

4. Borrow a patchwork quilt and share its history with the class. Explain why such quilts were popular in the olden days.

5. Interview teachers, classmates, and friends who are Native American (100% or less). Make a list of the various tribes represented and share one or two of their stories.

6. Write a story or poem about what the Turners or the Indians might have learned from their Christmas Eve experience.

THE DREAM AND THE CURSE OF SAM BRANNAN

1. Do you think a "curse" affected San Brannan's life? Why? Why not? What life choices might make a curse seem real?

2. Imagine you are Sam Brannan, editor of San Francisco's first newspaper. What stories are sure to sell papers? Explain why.

3. Make a list of Sam Brannan's virtues and flaws. Which list is longer? How did these things influence his life?

4. In what ways was Sam Brannan creative? Did others benefit from his creativity. Why? Why not?

5. Review a map and note what possible obstacles Sam Brannan faced when traveling from San Francisco to Sacramento.

6. What personal decisions might have led Brannan to a happier life?

THE SPIRIT OF JOAQUIN

1. In your opinion, what exactly is "the spirit of Joaquin?"

2. Write a brief story, poem, song or theatrical scene depicting Joaquin Murieta's and his bride's happy early life in California.

3. Why do you think Joaquin stayed in California? What else could he have done? Do you agree with his decision? Why? Why not?

4. List Joaquin's virtues and flaws. Describe a peaceful career in which he might have been successful. Explain why.

5. Why did Joaquin's gang members follow him? Describe other reasons why people follow leaders?

6. Memorize and recite a poem by Joaquin Miller, the famous poet who took Murieta's name.

THE SIEGE OF SEBASTOPOL

1. If the men at the Pine Grove store were living today, what issues do you think they would discuss?

2. If you owned the store in 1855 Pine Grove, what goods would you sell? Name ten modern grocery items that did not yet exist.

3. When Jeff Stevens and Charlie Hibbs felt personally insulted, they believed they had to "fight it out". In what other peaceful ways might they have solved their problem?

4. Create a poem, folk song or other type song about how Sebastopol, California got its name.

5. Think about your community and its qualities. If you were to rename your town, what would you call it? Explain why.

6. Imagine you are a TV reporter and describe the fight between Jeff Stevens and Charlie Hibbs.

LOLA MONTEZ AND LOTTA CRABTREE

1. Why do you think Lola's mother wanted her to marry an eighty-year-old man? List five to ten possible reasons. What is your opinion of such a marriage?

2. Name two modern performers who remind you of Lola and Lotta in seeking fame and fortune. How are they like Lola and Lotta?

3. Write a short story or script depicting the trial of Lola's bear.

4. Locate a song that Lola or Lotta might have sung or danced to. What does the song tell you about the 1850s?

5. In the 1850s, every town had a blacksmith. What work did blacksmiths perform and why were they important?

6. Do you think you would have enjoyed Lotta's life? Why? Why not?

A MOUNTAIN THAT WAS NAMED BY FATE

1. Have you been impressed by a mountain or other place in nature? Describe how it affected you, how you felt about it.

2. Draw or download flags or other symbols representing the people who, according to legend, named the mountain. Explain the symbolism on each flag to your classmates.

3. Imagine you are a traveler in 1841. Describe who you are, your journey (on foot, by horse or other means) and where you are headed.

4. Imagine you are Chief Solano. Describe to your village what you have seen and experienced.

5. Imagine you are the adventurous Russian princess, arguing why you should be allowed to climb mountains and take long rides in the wild countryside. Convince us or we won't let you go.

6. Write several entries in Captain Stephen Smith's log.

WILLIAM B. IDE, THE HERO OF SONOMA

1. Using a map, trace the Ide family's trip west.

2. Using the story's description, illustrate a picture of the Ide family as they begin their journey.

3. Find pictures of John C. Fremont, General Castro and General Vallejo to share with the class. Briefly describe each man.

4. List the factors that prompted Fremont's men to invade General Vallejo's home. What do you think you would have done in their situation?

5. What do you think California would be like if it had not become part of the United States? The same? Different? In what ways?

6. Would you like William Ide as a friend? Why? Why not?

SONTAG AND EVANS

1. If you have been hunting or camping and shared tall tales around the campfire, share one of the stories.

2. Folk stories are often exaggerated. Explain why you think this is so. How does exaggeration help or hurt a story?

3. List the reasons why Sontag and Evans hated the railroads and then list benefits the railroads provided. Suggest ways the hatred might have been avoided.

4. Why do you think Sontag and Evans robbed trains? Do you think they were folk heroes? Why? Why not?

5. Eva Evans is described as "mighty good lookin'". Find pictures of 1890s beauties. Compare that era's ideal beauty with today's.

6. The Sontag and Evans story became a 1914 movie melodrama. Describe some modern films based on actual events.

YOU CAN'T WIN 'EM ALL

1. Research and describe in detail the "Seven Deadly Sins".

2. On a map, track the travels of John Marsh. Approximately how many miles did he travel between Harvard and California?

3. List John Marsh's strengths and weaknesses. Do you think he used his talents effectively? Why? Why not?

4. Although John Marsh had no medical training, people went to him for medical care. Give reasons why you think they did this.

5. Imagine you work in Dr. Marsh's office. Using information in this story, create several different bills to patients for services rendered.

6. List instances where love was important. For each, do you think love was a positive or a negative influence? Why? Why not?

FIFTEEN SECONDS TO KILL

1. In your opinion, what were the real reasons the families in this story fought each other?

2. Were guns more harmful or more beneficial in this story? Compare and contrast this story to modern life?

3. Imagine you are a lawyer (prosecution or defense) for one of the families or individuals in this story. Present your case in class.

4. If the 1867 feud did begin with an argument about the Civil War, which family might have been for the North, which for the South? Use evidence from the story to back up your position.

5. Imagine you are one of the women who claimed the bodies of your men. Write a poem, song, letter or scene describing your feelings.

6. Write a love story based on the legendary romance between the Coates girl and Frost boy.

HIGH SPIRITS

1. Describe oldtimers you have observed sitting and watching the world go by. How do they behave? What do they talk about?

2. Describe you and your friends watching the passing scene.

3. Review the story and list every synonym for liquor (e.g., hootch). Then, make a list of modern terms for liquor. How many of the 1800s words are still in use today?

4. Do you think the characters in this story were respected by people who knew them? Would you respect or admire them? Why? Why not?

5. Look up the word "moonshine" in the encyclopedia and explain in detail where and how it originated.

6. Using research resources, draw a picture of a still and explain in precise detail how it works.

WHEN MALAY PETE WENT UP

1. Find Malasia (Malaya) on a map. Draw Pete's route to California and estimate how far he traveled.

2. Research the Malasian people of the mid-1800s. Draw a picture of what Malay Pete may have worn and carried with him to California.

3. List the strengths and weaknesses of Pete's flight preparations. What could he have done to ensure greater success?

4. Imagine you are a passenger in a hot-air balloon. Describe or draw in detail what you see looking down on your community.

5. Compare and contrast hot-air balloons of the 1800s to those of our modern era.

6. In what ways was Pete admirable and his failure magnificent?

LYNCHING AT LOOKOUT BRIDGE

1. Draw a picture using details in the first paragraph of this story.

2. List the community attitudes and actions that caused the Hall family to grow angry and strike back. For each negative attitude and action, suggest an action that might have had a positive influence.

3. Suppose in the year 2000 the ghost of the town marshal meets the ghost of a Hall family member. What would they say to each other?

4. Imagine you are one of the Hall women hiding on the hill during the hanging. Describe your feelings and thoughts.

5. Create a graph showing the evolution of Outlook's mob and ultimate violence.

6. Write a song or poem about the saga of Calvin Hall. Be sure to include facts in the last paragraph of the story.

ISHI

1. If you were to meet Ishi today, what things would you want him to see, experience and learn? Why?

2. Do you think social attitudes had changed for the better by the time Ishi was an adult? Why? Why not? If yes, what might have brought about the positive changes?

3. With a person who speaks a language you do not understand, try to communicate in his or her language. Write down words you learn.

4. Imagine you are Ishi leading the white man back to your home country. What are you feeling and thinking?

5. Design a book cover for a story about Ishi.

6. Write a short story in which you are the last living person of your race.

Notes

Notes

Story Locations Chart

Location by story	Train	Secret	Lady	Rain	Rock	Bart	Once	Sam	Joaquin	Siege	Lola	Fate	Ide	S&E	Win	15	High	Pete	Shad	Ishi
Adin																				
Altimira												X							X	
Alturas																			X	
American River								X												
Benicia			X																	
Bidwell Bar																			X	
Bieber											X									
Bodega										X		X								
Butte County					X															X
Butte Creek														X						
Calistoga								X				X								
Carmel									X											
Ceciliville		X							X											
Chico												X		X						
Clear Lake																				
Coffee Creek		X																		
Collis														X						

Location by story	Train	Secret	Lady	Rain	Rock	Bart	Once	Sam	Joaquin	Siege	Lola	Fate	Ide	S&E	Win	15	High	Pete	Shad	Ishi
Columbia						X														
Copperopolis						X														
Covelo						X														
Duncan's Mills						X														
Durham																				
ElCorado									X											
Escondido								X												
Eureka	X										X									
Fall River Valley						X	X													
Fort Ross			X			X				X		X								
Fort Crook							X												X	
Fresno														X						
Glendale				X																
Goose Lake							X													
Gouger's Neck																				
Grass Valley											X									
Guerneville				X		X														

Location by story	Train	Secret	Lady	Rain	Rock	Bart	Once	Sam	Joaquin	Siege	Lola	Fate	Ide	S&E	Win	15	High	Pete	Shad	Ishi
Happy Camp		X																		
Healdsburg																	X			
Hernet				X																
Lookout																			X	
Los Angeles				X									X		X					
Luffenholtz	X																			
Martinez													X							
Marysville		X							X											
McKinleyville															X					
Middletown																				
Monroeville													X							
Morena				X																
Mendocino Coast							X													
Mendocino County																X				
Mt. Shasta									X											
Mt. Diablo															X					
Napa Valley								X							X					

Location by story	Train	Secret	Lady	Rain	Rock	Bart	Once	Sam	Joaquin	Siege	Lola	Fate	Ide	S&E	Win	15	High	Pete	Shad	Ishi
Oroville						X					X			X				X		X
Otay				X																
Paradise Flat		X																		
Pine Grove										X										
Pit River							X													
Porterville														X						
Quincy											X									
Rabbit Creek				X							X									
Randsburg				X																
Red Bluff													X							
Redding																				X
Rich Bar											X									
Rough and Ready											X	X								
Russian River				X		X				X										
Sacramento River											X		X							
Sacramento								X												
Salmon River		X																		

Location by story	Train	Secret	Lady	Rain	Rock	Bart	Once	Sam	Joaquin	Siege	Lola	Fate	Ide	S&E	Win	15	High	Pete	Shad	Ishi
Sampson's Flat														X						
San Diego				X																
San Francisco			X		X	X		X			X	X	X							X
San Gabriel															X					
San Jose									X						X					
San Joaquin Valley														X						
San Joaquin River															X					
San Quentin															X					
San Rafael												X								
Santa Clara			X																	
Santa Rosa				X														X		
Sawyer's Bar		X																		
Scott Valley		X																		
Sebastopol										X										
Sierra Nevada								X	X				X					X		
Somes Bar		X																		
Sonoma											X	X	X		X					

Location by story	Train	Secret	Lady	Rain	Rock	Bart	Once	Sam	Joaquin	Siege	Lola	Fate	Ide	S&E	Win	15	High	Pete	Shad	Ishi
Sonoma County												X								
Sonora						X														
St. Helena												X								
Stockton						X			X											
Stone Corral														X						
Sutter's Fort													X							
Tehachapi Pass									X											
Tejon Pass									X											
Trinidad	X	X																		
Trinity Alps		X																		
Ukiah						X												X		
Visalia														X						
Weaverville		X				X					X									
Willits (Little Lake)																X				
Yuba River				X																
Yuba City				X				X												

About Rayve Productions

Rayve Productions is an award-winning small publisher of books and music. Current publications are primarily in the following categories:

> (1) Business guidebooks for home-based businesses and other entrepreneurs

> (2) Quality children's books and music, and parenting

> (3) History books about America and her regions, and an heirloom-quality journal for creating personal histories.

Rayve Productions' mail-order catalog offers the above items plus business books, software, music, and other enjoyable items produced by others.

Our ecletic collection of business resources and gift items has something to please everyone.

A FREE catalog is available upon request.

BUSINESS & CAREER

☆ *Smart Tax Write-offs: Hundreds of tax deduction ideas for home-based businesses, independent contractors, all entrepreneurs*
by Norm Ray, CPA

ISBN 1-877810-20-7, softcover, $12.95, 1996 pub.

Fun-to-read, easy-to-use guidebook that encourages entrepreneurs to be aggressive and creative in taking legitimate tax deductions. Includes valuable checklist of over 600 write-off ideas. Every small business owner's "must read." (Recommended by *Home Office Computing, Small Business Opportunities, Spare Time, Independent Business Magazine*).

☆ *The Independent Medical Transcriptionist, 3rd edition: The comprehensive guidebook for career success in a home-based medical transcription business* by Donna Avila-Weil, CMT and Mary Glaccum, CMT

ISBN 1-877810-23-1, softcover, $34.95, 1998 pub.

The industry's premier reference book for medical transcription entrepreneurs. (Recommended by *Journal of the American Association for Medical Transcription, Entrepreneur, Small Business Opportunities*)

☆ *Independent Medical Coding: The comprehensive guidebook for career success as a home-based medical coder*
by Donna Avila-Weil, CMT and Rhonda Regan, CCS

ISBN 1-877810-17-7, softcover, $34.95, 1998 pub.

How to start and successfully run your own professional independent medical coding business. Step-by-step instructions.

☆ *Easy Financials for Your Home-based Business*   by Norm Ray, CPA

ISBN 1-877810-92-4, softcover, $19.95, 1992 pub.

Small business & home-based business expert helps you save time by making your work easier, and save money by nailing down your tax deductions. (Recommended by *Wilson Library Bulletin, The Business Journal, National Home Business Report*)

☆ *Internal Medicine Words*   by Minta Danna

ISBN 1-877810-68-1, softcover, $29.95, 1997 pub.

Over 8,000 words and terms related to internal medicine. A valuable spelling and terminology usage resource for medical transcriptionists, medical writers and editors, court reporters, medical records personnel, and others working with medical documentation.

☆ *Shrinking the Globe into Your Company's Hands: The step-by-step international trade guide for small businesses*   by Sidney R. Lawrence, PE

ISBN 1-877810-46-0, softcover, $24.95, 1997 pub.

An expert in foreign trade shows U.S. small business owners how to market and export products and services safely and profitably.

HISTORY

☆ *20 Tales of California: A rare collection of western stories* by Hector Lee
ISBN 1-877810-62-2, softcover, $9.95, 1998 pub.
Mysterious and romantic tales: real life and folklore set in various California locations. Includes ideas for family outings and classroom field trips.

☆ *Link Across America: A story of the historic Lincoln Highway* — see Children's Books

☆ *Windsor, The Birth of a City*   by Gabriel A. Fraire
ISBN 1-877810-91-6, hardcover, $21.95, 1991 pub.
Fascinating case study of political and social issues surrounding city incorporation of Windsor, California, 1978—1991. LAFCO impact.

☆ *LifeTimes, The Life Experiences Journal*
ISBN 1-877810-34-7, hardcover, $49.95
World's easiest, most fun and useful personal journal. Handsome heirloom quality with gilt-edged pages. Over 150 information categories to record your life experiences. Winner of national award for excellence.

GENERAL

☆ *Nancy's Candy Cookbook: How to make candy at home the easy way*
                                                            by Nancy Shipman
ISBN 1-877810-65-7, softcover, $14.95, 1996 pub.
Have fun and save money by making candy at home at a fraction of candy store prices. More than 100 excellent candy recipes — from Grandma's delicious old-fashioned fudge to modern gourmet truffles. Includes many children's favorites, too.

☆ *Joy of Reading: One family's fun-filled guide to reading success*
                                                            by Debbie Duncan
ISBN 1-877810-45-2, softcover, $14.95, 1998 pub.
A dynamic author and mother, and an expert on children's literature, shares her family's personal reading success stories. You'll be inspired and entertained by this lighthearted, candid glimpse into one family's daily experiences as they cope with the ups and downs of life. Through it all, there is love, and an abundance of wonderful books to mark the milestones along the way.

CHILDREN'S BOOKS & MUSIC

☆ *Link Across America: A story of the historic Lincoln Highway*
by Mary Elizabeth Anderson
ISBN 1-877810-97-5, hardcover, $14.95, 1997 pub.
It began with a long-ago dream ... a road that would run clear across America! The dream became reality in 1914 as the Lincoln Highway began to take form, to eventually run from New York City to San Francisco. Venture from past to present experiencing transportation history. Topics include Abraham Lincoln, teams of horses, seedling miles, small towns, making concrete, auto courts, Burma Shave signs, classic cars and road rallies. Color photos along today's Lincoln Highway remnants, b/w historical photos, map and list of cities along the old Lincoln Highway. (Ages 7-13 & their parents, grandparents & great-grandparents)

☆ *The Perfect Orange: A tale from Ethiopia*
by Frank P. Araujo, PhD; illustrated by Xiao Jun Li
ISBN 1-877810-94-0, hardcover, $16.95, 1994 pub., Toucan Tales volume 2
Inspiring gentle folktale. Breathtaking watercolors dramatize ancient Ethiopia's contrasting pastoral charm and majesty. Illustrations are rich with Ethiopian details. Story reinforces values of generosity and selflessness over greed and self-centeredness. Glossary of Ethiopian terms and pronunciation key.
(**PBS** *Storytime* **Selection**; Recommended by *School Library Journal, Faces, MultiCultural Review, Small Press Magazine, The Five Owls, Wilson Library Bulletin*)

☆ *Nekane, the Lamiña & the Bear: A tale of the Basque Pyrenees*
by Frank P. Araujo, PhD; illustrated by Xiao Jun Li
ISBN 1-877810-01-0, hardcover, $16.95, 1993 pub., Toucan Tales volume 1
Delightful Basque folktale pits appealing, quick-witted young heroine against mysterious villain. Lively, imaginative narrative, sprinkled with Basque phrases. Vibrant watercolor images. Glossary of Basque terms and pronunciation key.
(Recommended by School Library Journal, Publishers Weekly, Kirkus Reviews, Booklist, Wilson Library Bulletin, The Basque Studies Program Newsletter: University of Nevada, BCCB, The Five Owls)

☆ *The Laughing River: A folktale for peace*
by Elizabeth Haze Vega; illustrated by Ashley Smith, 1995 pub.
ISBN 1-877810-35-5   hardcover book, $16.95
ISBN 1-877810-36-3   companion musical audiotape, $9.95
ISBN 1-877810-37-1   book & musical audiotape combo, $23.95
Drum kit, $9.95
Book, musical audiotape & drum kit combo, $29.95
Two fanciful African tribes are in conflict until the laughing river bubbles melodiously into their lives, bringing fun, friendship, peace. Lyrical fanciful folktale of conflict resolution. Mesmerizing music. Dancing, singing and drumming instructions. Orff approach. (Recommended by *School Library Journal*)

☆ *When Molly Was in the Hospital: A book for brothers and sisters of hospitalized children*
> by Debbie Duncan; illustrated by Nina Ollikainen, MD

ISBN 1-877810-44-4, hardcover, $12.95, 1994 pub.

Anna's little sister, Molly, has been very ill and had to have an operation. Anna tells us all about the experience from her point of view. Sensitive, insightful, heartwarming story. A support and comfort for siblings and those who love them. Authentic. Realistic. Effective.

(Winner of 1995 Benjamin Franklin Award: Best Children's Picture Book. Recommended by *Children's Book Insider, School Library Journal, Disabilities Resources Monthly*)

☆ *Night Sounds*
> by Lois G. Grambling; illustrated by Randall F. Ray

ISBN 1-877810-77-0, hardcover, $12.95   ISBN 1-877810-83-5, softcover, $6.95, 1996 pub.

Perfect bedtime story. Ever so gently, a child's thoughts slip farther and farther away, moving from purring cat at bedside and comical creatures in the yard to distant trains and church bells, and then at last, to sleep. Imaginative, lilting text and daringly unpretentious b/w watercolor illustrations

☆ *Los Sonidos de la Noche*
> by Lois G. Grambling; illustrated by Randall F. Ray

(Spanish edition of *Night Sounds*), 1996 pub.

ISBN 1-877810-76-2, hardcover, $12.95   ISBN 1-877810-82-7, softcover, $6.95

ORDER

For mail orders please complete this order form and forward with check, money order or credit card information to Rayve Productions, POB 726, Windsor CA 95492. If paying with a credit card, you can call us toll-free at 800.852.4890 or fax this completed form to Rayve Productions at 707.838.2220.

You can also order at our web site at www.spannet.org/rayve.

☐ Please send me the following book(s):

Title _____ Price _____ Qty ____ Amount _____

Title _____ Price _____ Qty ____ Amount _____

Title _____ Price _____ Qty ____ Amount _____

Title _____ Price _____ Qty ____ Amount _____

Total Amount _____

Sales Tax: Californians please add 7.5% sales tax   Sales Tax _____

S/H: Book rate --- $3 for first book + $.50 each additional   Shipping _____

Priority --- $4 for first book + $.75 each additional

Total _____

Name _____   Phone _____

Address _____

City State Zip _____

☐ Check enclosed $ _____   Date _____

☐ Charge my Visa/MC/Discover/AMEX $ _____

Credit card # _____   Exp. _____

Signature _____   *Thank you!*